Schizophrenic Episode

Series

Amy Pener
MS
Psychology

Amy Perez MS
Psychology

Published in 2018

Copyright 2019

ISBN: 9781674748030

Printed by Amazon

Front Cover Design by Author.

Book Design by Designer.

Author: Amy Perez MS Psychology

https://www.amazon.com/kindle-dbs/author/ref=dbs_P_W_auth?_encoding=UTF8&author=Amy%20Perez%20MS%20Psychology&searchAlias=digital-text&asin=B07H24NKYJ

Episode 1

1

"Excuse me sir! Are you okay?"

Who is that talking? I look up in the night sky. They are coming for me. I know it.

"Sir, is that your car smashed down the road?" I gotta run! I throw my cigarette into the grass and take off into the field. They will never get me. My chest is pounding. My body is aching. Blood is dripping from my forehead and elbows. I gotta get outta here man. I gotta find my brother. He can get me out of this mess. He was always good at fleeing the scene.

"Sir, stand down."

No way man! I grip my cigarettes in my front pocket. "Sir! You are surrounded!" Oh yeah? Watch this asshole!

I turn around to see six blurred figures surrounding me. Too bad they are no match for me. I grew up in the south boys. I can wrestle anyone in the grass. Three of you are too overweight to even catch me. I might not be the strongest, but I'm quick. As lightning.

First comes a left hook. Contact. Yep they don't stand a chance. Next a right kick to chubby's cheek. Take that asshole. You think you can really mess with me? Two short men approach me. One has a black shiny stick in his hand. I grab their necks and throw their heads together. They crumple to the ground. Goodnight boys!

This has got to be a joke. A tall skinny guy with red hair approaches me. He is wearing a blue shirt and slacks. You think you can take me huh? Take your chance young man. My knees are bent. My fists are out right in front of my face. Whoever he is, he is about to meet his friends on the ground. They can't mess with me! I'm King David!

2

Come on slim! Show me whatcha got. I don't have all night now. If these aliens show up, I'll be the least of your problems. God has sent them. It's the only way. Why do you think I'm here? I'm going to save us all. I have to. For my girls. Carrie and Dana need to have a good life. These alien cocksuckers are not getting to my family. Just wait until I get to their headquarters.

A skinny left arm swings by my face as I dodge it. I let out a wild laugh. I should just let the kid go. The other guys were cocky. They deserved it. But him? He's just a kid. A child. He reminds me of me. I used to be a little guy. I was skinny with red hair and freckles. I was a shrimp in comparison to my older brother. He was gigantic. Which is why I need to find him. I'm locked eye to eye with the kid.

Maybe we can meet at an agreement here. We can reason with each other. He's young. He might be easily manipulated. Not that he needs to be. These huge aliens are going to wipe us all out. There is a secret agency that has been protecting us but they are failing. Aliens are coming from everywhere.

"Come on kid, just let me go, and we can both walk away from this," I beg. I don't want to hurt him. I hear some groaning from the ground. It's chubby. I kick him in his stomach. Stay down.

"Sir, I can't do that." He reaches for something in his belt. A knife? A gun?

"You don't understand slim. They are coming for us. Any minute now there is going to be aliens everywhere."

The kid lets out a loud laugh. Really? You think it's funny? It won't be funny when they suck the eyeballs out of your head.

3

I fake a punch at his face with my left hand and swing my right leg back and boom! Round house kick to the temple. Whoops. Sorry kid. I really didn't want to. His skinny body crumples to the ground. I check his belt. What was he reaching for? There is nothing there. Hhmm. Weird. I see something shining in the grass. I walk over and peer at the object. Shit. It's a gun.

I'm not trying to take any lives here. The last time I shot a gun was when I was sixteen. I was in the backwoods of Tennessee. My Pa taught my brother and I how to shoot a shot gun. Even though my brother was ten years older than me, I could always keep up. If Anthony shot a peasant, I would shoot two. I could always one up him. Sometimes he would let it slide and sometimes he would get mad and competitive. Sometimes we would end up in the grass to fight it out.

"Goddammit boys! Knock that shit out!" My Pa would shout at us. He tried his best but the alcohol would take over him. It turned him into a monster. You couldn't even recognize him. You wouldn't wanna piss him off. He took it all out on my Ma though. I lost count of how many times I visited her in the hospital. Bruises and cuts would cover her body.

I pick up the small handgun from the grass. I put it into my back pocket. This could come in handy. I don't want to use it but if I have to I will. I might need to pistol whip chubby if he tries to get up. I reach for my front pocket. Phew. My cigarettes are still there. My menthols. My lifesaver. As long as we have the cigarettes, we are good to go. I just wish I had an ice-cold pop to go with my smoke. I grip my cigarette pack and stare down at the six bodies lying around me. Nice try boys. No one is going to stop me. I must protect my little girls. Two Teethers and Pumpkin.

4

I take out the soft pack of cigarettes from the pocket of my blue shirt. Almost a full pack. I pull out a one hundred. I take the Bic lighter in my hand and light up my cigarette. My mouth fills with smoke. I don't inhale though. I never inhale. Only an idiot would do that. Why would you fill your lungs up with all of those chemicals? I'm not stupid.

I studied at the seminary after high school. I was the top of my class. I was teaching the pastors all about the bible. I had read the bible over one hundred times. There was nothing they couldn't teach me. I may not always preach the bible to everyone but I act like a believer. I kick some gravel as I walk down the road. I ash my cigarette into the grass. I take another hit. The

menthol fills my mouth. I gotta get to Anthony.
We can be a team.

Anthony is the only person I can trust with
this mission. It will be him and I against the
aliens. I saw the master alien before I crashed
my damn car. I just bought that car too.
Elizabeth was pissed. She didn't understand why
I came home with a brand-new car. She didn't
understand. How do you explain to your wife
and kids that our world is going to end? There
was no time for words. I remember my wife
screaming as I was getting into the car. I was
trying to bring our dog as my copilot. But she
was screaming at the top of her lungs.

I know I was angry but she didn't
understand. There was no time to explain. I told
her that Elliot and I had a mission. It wasn't a lie.
But Elliot the sheep dog wasn't coming home. I

was tired of him shitting all over my house. And the scratching. He would scratch all day and night without stop. I just couldn't take any more of that damn dog. Until I found his purpose. He was going to have a front row seat to the end of the world. With me.

5

I take a drag off of my cigarette and fill my mouth full of smoke. There is a chill in the air. It's fall in the North. It's right around Carrie's birthday. My little Pumpkin. She's only seven years old. She has golden blonde hair. She's an angel. Dana is growing so fast. They need their Dad to be a hero. Elizabeth doesn't get it. This problem is bigger than us.

She doesn't understand me. I work ninety hours a week to put food on the table. All she cares about are her damn animals. She could try and care more about me than a bunch of animals. Ten pets is too much. I can feel my forehead wrinkled in anger. I needed to get out of there. I couldn't take it anymore. I was just going to clear my head. Until I saw him.

God. He came to me. He spoke to me of the invasion. It was a message for me. I was on a back road in my small town. Next thing I know I'm here. Where here is, I have no idea. I need to find a street sign or something. It's so dark out. Maybe I should walk back and find my car. Those men should be gone by now. They really didn't see that coming did they? A smile crosses my face. I'm pretty quick.

My brother is in Georgia so if I could just get there and explain everything to him, we will be good to go. I got enough cash in my pocket to get there. I can take a bus. But first I better stock up on smokes. I take a long drag off my cigarette. God, I could use a little guidance right about now. Whatcha got? 1992 is turning out to be an interesting year so far. Ow! Dammit! What was that? I see red as my body hits the dirt road.

6

It's chubby. My hands are handcuffed behind me as I struggle to get out. He was a cop. They were all cops. This isn't good. Not at all. I need to call Elizabeth. Chubby gives me a nasty look. He has a big black eye and a bloody lip. "Yes, we are processing him right here. Do you want us to hold him here or bring him tonight?" A young woman with black hair is on the phone. She stares at me with a concerned look on her face.

I look down at my front pocket. Dammit. My cigarettes. Their gone. I need my smokes. A Coca Cola would be nice too. My mouth is filled with a dry feeling. My head is pounding. How did I get here? My eyes feel like they are wide open. Like I couldn't close them if I tried. My muscles are filled with adrenaline. The chubby cop just stands there staring at me. Who's the big man now is what he's probably thinking. Yeah, he is pretty sour over the fact that I took him and his buddies out.

They came up to me. They interrupted my mission. Don't mess with a man on a mission. As soon as we clear this up, I can get back to my business. Who do these people think they are? You can't just sneak up on a young man in the middle of the night like that. They made me drop my cigarette. "Okay, thank you." The dark-haired woman hangs up the phone.

"Mr. Clark, we are going to hold you here overnight in isolation and tomorrow you will be transferred to the Columbia Correctional Institution."

I stare at her blankly. Chubby is munching on a cheeseburger as his mouth parts open in a smirk. Then he busts out laughing exposing a mouthful of chewed food. I've had enough of this asshole. The cop comes closer to me. I jump up and head-butt him in the chin as hard as I can.

7

He falls like a ton of bricks to the floor. That'll teach him. I'm immediately rushed to the ground. It was worth it. That guy had it comin'.

"Mr. Clark! Stay down sir. Do not attempt to move." A voice is yelling in my ear. All I see is red. My vision goes blurry.

"Andrew can you hear me? I am with the Wisconsin State Police. Do not attempt to move." I feel a piece of steel pressed against the back of my head.

They don't understand. This problem is bigger than us. We are slowly getting invaded. The aliens are not going to back down. I need to get to my brother Anthony. Tonight. I feel cold metal clank around my ankles. There are two men with their knees pressed against my back. I can't see a way out of this one. Shit. A need a sign God. What do I do now? I'm lifted up by three men and dragged down a hallway filled with cells. The beige paint is being chipped away from the metal bars. The floor is covered in a dusty film.

The men drag my body into a cell. My head bangs into a metal toilet. I can smell a strong scent of urine. The metal doors slam behind me. My feet and hands are completely locked up. I can't move. My face is pressed against the damp dirty floor. My breathing is labored. There is a pounding in my chest. My blood is pumping so hard that it feels like my veins are going to burst. My eyes are burning.

My cell door whips open. In a flash I feel kicks all over my body. Black boots stomp the floor after each wail. I'm wincing in pain. I feel each bone getting hit. More like crushed. Dammit. Shit. I'm dying tonight. What have I done? I'm so sorry Two Teethers and Pumpkin.

Daddy tried to save the world. I did everything I could. Daddy loves you.

8

I look up to see a barred window. Small slivers of sun shines through. Parts of my body are numb. Others feel so achy that I can't move. I lick my lips to taste that familiar iron flavor. Blood. There is a pool of blood and saliva on the dirty floor below my face. I can hear men talking and laughing in the distance. My wrists and ankles are still shackled together. My mouth feels like a desert. All I can smell is urine. I hear thick boots hitting the floor towards my cell.

"You put Mikey in the hospital you know Mr. Clark." My mouth is too dry to speak. That bastard is probably happy. Free vacation. He'll lay around for a month and collect a disability payment. He'll be fine. He deserves worse for how he was antagonizing me. That man knew what he was doing. He tried to piss me off on purpose. More importantly, I need a cigarette. Like now.

"You're getting transferred in a bit Mr. Clark. Don't you worry. We're gonna put you over with the big guys."

The big guys huh? Are they bigger than you? Because I'm not too worried then.

"Oh, and we spoke to your wife, she is too far to make it right now to bail you out."

Elizabeth isn't going to understand any of this. What in the hell were we fighting about anyways? She really is a good wife. And the mother of my children. Why does she make me so angry sometimes? How did I end up in Wisconsin? They are our neighboring state. I was trying to go south over to Georgia. After the image God sent me everything is such a blur. This urine smell is so toxic. I wriggle my body to lay in a different direction.

Three men approach my cell. "Mr. Clark." We're here to take you to the big house."

The cell door whips open. The men grab both of my arms while my body is dragged into a plastic chair. Chains are attached to each ankle as the previous cuffs are removed. The officers stand me up.

"Come with us." I limp along with the officers. I definitely have a broken bone or two.

9

They are cleaning out the cell. I can smell the bleach. It reminds me of the time with my victims. All of the body parts are still fresh in my mind. The sex. My power. I can still feel the power I had over them. Yeah because you drugged them. Shut up! Shut up! You don't know anything. They wanted it. They just didn't know it. They wanted to be dominated by me.

I paid them the fifty bucks. If only I could go back and finish my alter. I would have ten skulls. I could be reclining back right now staring at my work. It took years to obtain all of those bones. And the taste. I just can't get the flavor out of my head. The human flesh. The muscle. The skin. I loved fileting the muscle from the bone. The process. There is a hardening between my legs. Every day I relive them and it's torturous. I want to be back out there.

Apartment 214 was where they were. Night after night of fun. I miss the alcohol. I wish I had a shot and a beer right about now. I miss the alcohol. But I miss the sex and the flesh more. If I could just have one more of them. One more taste. The muscles were tough but I could perfect the preparation process. I just needed more time. My time was cut short by the one that got away. My big mistake. If it wasn't for the last boy, I would have my alter of skulls right now. I already had nine.

"Right this way Mr. Clark. Your cell is ready for you."

Ah who is this? Fresh meat? He's handsome. Mr. Clark huh? He has thick brown hair and a nice build.

"Can I get a cigarette please?"

"I'll see what I can do Andrew."

Nice name too. Andrew. I like it. He has nice blue eyes to go with it. He is much more handsome than any of the other men. I would love to eat his heart out. "Time for a shower Gavin." My cell swings open just in time to get one last look. Hi Andrew.

Schizophrenic Episode Series

Episode 2

1

I finally got my thirty minutes a day. If only I could get some alcohol. I'll have to settle for a shower. It's hard being locked away for twenty-three hours. My mind is going crazy.

"Ten minutes Gavin." The guard is direct and assertive. He reminds me of my Father. Where is he now? I need him now more than ever. He didn't care about me before. Shit! The water comes out so cold. I don't have enough time. I need to mull some things over. I need the water to scald my skin. I deserve to burn for what I've done. Although I'm sorry, I can't take away the urges. I feel like the devil. The devil himself spawned me. I can't get the taste of the flesh out of my mind it's intoxicating.

"Five minutes sir." Goddammit! I need more time than this. Electricity surges through my veins. I just want to fry myself in this water. I want it to be over. I want these impulses to end. What's wrong with me? "Water off Gavin." I didn't even get enough warmth. I need to feel alive. The only thing that makes me feel alive is the flesh. The blood. I dry off my thin body. I won't last in here.

Many of the men are large in here. I could never subdue them. Not without drugs. I am weak in here. I don't have my weapons.

"Right this way Mr. Clark." Mr. Clark again. Why is he here? He doesn't fit the cliché of the men in here. He's different. It was in his face, his demeanor. I peak my head from the shower. I see a large silhouette of a man being led through the showers. His ankles are chained.

He must have done something serious. Could he be as bad as me? Worse? Dammit. I need a drink. I'll take a nice shot and a cold beer.

"Sir would you like to make any calls or play basketball?"

The guard is big and thick. His light skin is met with freckles and red hair. Basketball? Is there alcohol out there? I'm dying for a drink. I yearn for a taste of blood as well. I could subdue the guard outside. He's not my type though. But a kill could get rid of the voices. Even for a moment. They keep haunting me. There is a monster inside me. I have to let him out.

"No, I'll go back to my cell."

2

"Would you like some shampoo Mr. Clark?"

Shampoo? No. I don't want shampoo. I want to go home. I want my kids.

"No thank you." Why am I here? I'm not supposed to be here. Who can get me out of this? If I don't complete my mission, we are all screwed. I rub the soap on my body. I can't remember when I last showered. The water offers some clarity as the blood washes off my body. God? Can you come to me? I need some answers. What do I do next? I won't abandon the mission. I will complete it at all costs. Even if I have to get through all of these people. My little girls need me. They need their Daddy to do what's right. I just want to see their smiles again. My Pumpkin and Two Teethers.

I have to accept that I may never see them again. I knew when I accepted this mission that it was a one-way ticket. Elizabeth wouldn't understand. She didn't grow up the way I did. She had the perfect life. Her parents live on a lake. They gave her a life that I could never dream of. All of the parties. All of the endless celebrations. She never saw her Mom get beat to a pulp. She never saw a drunk man stumble in every night. She doesn't understand what we went through. My siblings and I never had a home. We moved around so much. We were always at the mercy of the next landlord.

Why can't she see what I'm trying to do? I want my little girls to have a good life. I want them to have everything I didn't. Even if it costs me my life. I would do anything for those little girls. I want them to see. What do they think I work ninety hours a week for? My job. I need to speak to them. I need to explain. If I don't complete this mission, my job won't be there anymore. I have until Devil's Night. The aliens have given us an ultimatum. Bring them The Word of God or this world is going to burn.

I'm going to give them The Word of God alright. I know first-hand how mighty he is. God came to me when I was only five. After falling off the back of our porch he came to me. He gave me three months in a coma to show me. They only had to drill three holes in my head. I remember it like it was yesterday. My Ma stayed in the garden for hours. She picked tomaters and green beans. I can practically smell her cooking. She was so busy, she missed me falling off of the porch.

3

I would do anything for a slice of her cornbread. Skillet style. She made that cornbread so thick and rich.

"Five minutes Mr. Clark."

Wow. This the longest shower I've had in a while. I was always in a rush. Those two little girls keep me so busy. I can barely use the bathroom and brush my teeth, much less shower. They are the reason for everything. What's next God? Tell me what to do? Do I stay here? Do I flee? What's the next part of the mission? If I don't get to the meeting slot before Halloween, our world is doomed. I need to get ahold of my brother. He needs to know. We are being punished for our actions.

What did we think someone would think of us? All of our sinning, our greed. Aliens from other planets have been watching us. They are not happy. But I can prove them wrong. I just need The Word of God. Will they want to see a bible? Will my word be enough?

"Water off Andrew, dry off and get out. You can play some basketball or make a phone call."

The walls of this shower are caked with dirt and mold. I'll be lucky not to catch an infection in here. My years as a custodian have taught me enough to know that these conditions could be deadly. Does anyone clean this place? I grab the towel from the hook. It's tainted brown. I dry off my hair and try to wrap it around my waist. It's too small. This is humiliating.

I open the small green curtain when I see it. His eyes. Their red. Supernatural. They've infiltrated the facility. The aliens. His hair is red and his eyes are too. And he has gills. He is not human. God has shown up. I must take him down and escape. I am quick. He's a big man but I can take him. As soon as he turns around, I will strike. He must have some super powers though. I have to do this though. For my girls.

Here's my chance. I can see the veins in the side of his neck pulsing. He's not human. No one has eyes that red color. These aliens are satanic. The Word of God may not even get through to them. I could choke him out. Or strike him in the back of the head. Then I can make a run for it. All of the sudden I feel metal shackles clasp to my ankles. The red eyed alien reaches back and hand cuffs me.

4

Too late. If I take out big red, I could lose valuable information. I need to find out all I can from these people. What do they want? Will the word of God reach them?

"Do you want to go out in the yard or make a phone call?"

I should call Elizabeth. She won't understand though. I don't want a lecture. I don't want to hear her get upset with me. She will understand at the end. It's better to ask for forgiveness than permission on this one.

"I'll step outside," I reply to the guards. "I could go for a smoke if ya got one." Silence. Fat chance of getting a cigarette in this joint. I have been reduced to an animal. Or a possession. They have taken over my body but they won't take my mind.

No one will ever take my mind.

"Sir we are going to put you in a cell around the corner to change." The guards lead my naked body to a cell. It's dark and dingy. My skin is still moist from the shower. The guard takes off my cuffs. The red eyes. Where is he from? Why is he here? Has he come for me? He won't stop my mission. I don't care who or what he is.

"Do you read the bible?" I ask him. There is a long pause.

"I'll get you a cigarette and some clothes," he sighs. Have I reached a common ground with him?

Have they heard of the good book? Do they know of Jesus? I feel cold, moist and shriveled up. The cold bars offer little comfort. My wet feet swipe across the dirty floor. Feces stains the metal toilet in the cell. There is a brown stained mattress. My body surges with disgust. This is torture. Big Red returns with a stack of clothing, pair of sandals and a perfect looking cigarette. There really is a God. He has just shown me a sign.

I can get through to them. If I can show them the word then they will know that us humans are good. Maybe I am in this place for a reason. My next step is to get a bible. I need to show them. I need to teach them. I might be coming home girls. This mission was interrupted for a reason. This fortress is the new meeting place. Everything happens for a reason. I set my cigarette on the stained mattress. I slip on the orange pants on over my damp legs. I slip on the plastic sandals. I slide the orange shirt over my head. There is a perfect sized square pocket on the left side of the shirt. A perfect place for my smoke. I slide the cigarette into my pocket.

5

I'm ready to go outside. I need a taste of freedom. Big Red comes to my cell. A short dark-haired man walks up behind him. He has the shackles in his hands.

"Can we trust you to just shackle your legs?" The short man asks. His white teeth glimmer through his dark skin. He trusts me. Is he one of them? Are they from the same planet? We are going to have a meeting here aren't we? But they have to make sure that they can trust me. I didn't exactly make a good impression when they abducted me did I? It's not my fault. They attacked me. These people caught me off guard.

"I'll behave," I lie. No promises. If I get a sign that I need to do something drastic, I will. The world is depending on me.

They need me in a big way. The short man opens the cell and walks over and shackle my ankles. They lead me out of the shower area and through old metal doors. The rust is taking over the edges. The plastic sandals are uncomfortable between my toes. My feet slide while they are cuffed together. This is my new normal. Like an animal I am led to the outdoors. A small red door leads to the outside.

The ground is damp. There is a small yard with an old basketball court. The net is hanging down. Yellow, red and orange trees surround a metal fence. Barbed wire is curved high to keep us in. Or is it to keep people out? I step out into the wet grass. I breath in the damp, cold fall air. It's almost Pumpkin's birthday I am here for a reason. I have to make sure she has many more birthdays. I hope she understands. Daddy had to.

I reach into my shirt pocket. I grab the long cigarette. This is Elizabeth's fault. I never smoked before I met her. She kept pressuring me. She didn't want to smoke by herself at her parent's lake house. I would do anything for her, doesn't she see that? But six cats and a dog is too much. I can't take it anymore. I didn't grow up that way. I had a dog once. Spot, a small beagle. My Pa took one look at him and took him for a walk. Spot never came back. Anthony and I both heard the gunshot in the distance. My Pa didn't have patience for a dog. Or any animal.

6

It is kind of ironic that now I am basically an animal, the way they drag me around this place. I have no rights. No freedom. My metal shackles drag between my legs as I check out the yard.

"Yo Andrew!" The short guard yells from the doors. He has a big white smile with gapped teeth. And something beautiful and yellow in his hand. A lighter. I start walking towards him as fast as my shackles let me. He meets me half way. "Man, what are you doing in here Andrew?" He lights the lighter towards my cigarette. I put it to my lips and breath in the flame. The end of my cigarette lights in a ball of fire as the tobacco shrivels up. I inhale the smoke deep into my lungs.

I never inhale but I need the high from the nicotine in here.

"You don't want to know," I tell him. I don't want him to fear me. I need him to hear the word. The word of God can heal all of us. I should know, I've read the bible countless times.

"What's your name boss?" I exhale the cigarette smoke away from his face.

"James sir, my name's James. I'm up here from Alabama." I take another puff off of my smoke.

"You're a long way from home ain't ya?" He's lying. My ass he's from Alabama. He made it up on the fly. I'm not leaving this yard, am I? I probably have until I finish this cigarette and my time is up. I know too much.

James smiles and walks back towards the door. He stands in front of the door with his arms crossed. He looks up at the sky. Where are they at boss? They're coming, aren't they? I take one more puff of my smoke. The smoke fills up my lungs. I never inhale. This is a special occasion though. I exhale the smoke and toss my lit cigarette in the grass.

"What do you want from me?" I yell into the sky. "Come and get me you assholes!" I throw my hands up in the air. "Do what you want to me!" Just don't take me girls. I'll give you what you want. I don't need a bible. The Word is all in my brain.

"Hey Andrew man, you aight over there?" James shouts out to me.

Do I look alright to you boss? I feel drops of water on my face. It's time. I bend down and then fall into the wet grass. Just do it already. Beam me up. I close my eyes tight. This is going to hurt. The rain drops fall on my face. This is for you girls. I'm doing it all for you. I hear footsteps trampling through the grass. I open my eyes to see Big Red and James. A needle stabs into my left thigh. A dizziness takes over my brain and I fade away.

7

"Just put him back in his cell man." Who is that getting dragged down the hall?

"What are they doing out there?" The guards seem upset.

"I don't know man; he was yelling at the sky and then he fell in the grass. He was hysterical."

Hi Andrew. His lifeless body is dragging by my cell. If only I could get ahold of the drugs they have in here. I would like to sedate somebody like that. Andrew's head drags on the floor as they drag him by his shackled feet. I'm feeling quite turned on by this situation. If only we had a joint cell. This night could be more fun than normal. Oh hello Mr. Andrew. We will be meeting soon. I practically feel a knife stabbing through his muscle.

I can feel the blood trickle down my arm. So warm. Andrew we are going to be the best of friends. I want to learn everything about you. Where are you from? How did you get here? The cold metal doors to his cell slam shut. The police took everything from me. I almost had enough human skulls to make a full alter. What was I thinking letting that last guy get away? He stopped the monster. But the monster is inside of me. He will never go away. It's because you are a sinner! Shut up! Shut the fuck up! You don't know me! I have to let the monster out. I need blood. I need flesh.

"Gavin, your dinner is here." A young pretty woman yells from down the hall.

"Thank you, Monica." If I liked women, she would be my pick. Her long dark hair covers her breasts just so. She has perfect lips and long legs. She is thick in all the right places. If I looked like her, I would be more accepted. She walks up with a big smile.

"I see you got a shower today." Barely. I wouldn't call that cold water shit a shower.

"How are you feeling today?"

How am I feeling? How the fuck do you think I'm feeling? I'm an animal. A monster.

"I'm good, ya got any beer?"

Monica lets out a big laugh. She is so easy. She's easy to talk to. She smiles easy. And her laugh. It's infectious.

Her perfume hits my nose from outside my cell.

"I wish," she replies through her laughter. "You sure are charming Gavin." She unlocks a tiny door that is large enough to slip my tray through. Ugh. Meatloaf. It's the worst meal in this place. It's not like my Grandma's. At least I had her. My parents may not have been around but at least she seemed to accept me. Even though she didn't approve of me with the men, she still let it happen.

"Thank you, Monica." Her soft skin looks like a dream compared to my littered brain. I wish I could trade places with her. The men would flock to me. Society would accept me. I wouldn't have to hide anymore.

8

I set the tray down on my bed. The green beans are watery. The mashed potatoes look like clay. The roll is hard as a rock. I'm forgotten

● ● ●

about. I'm being left here to rot. You deserve it for what you've done! Shut up! Shut the fuck up! I can't keep the monster inside forever. "Aaahh!" I swing my tray around sending the disgusting food flying all over my cell. The meatloaf smashes against the wall. Mashed potatoes hit the ceiling. "Shut the fuck up! I can't take it anymore!"

I bash my tray against the metal cell bars. Over and over. Get out of my head! Damn you! Monica comes running down the hall. She takes one look at me and runs back the other way. Shit. The one person that was nice to me. Now she knows. I can't hide anymore. Footsteps come pounding down the hall. A group of men armed with nightsticks line the front of my cell. "I'm going to let him out!" I scream at the top of my lungs. "He's coming out!" The guards have helmets on and shields in front of them. They can't stop the monster. No matter how hard they try, he won't go away. Nobody can stop this.

"Gavin, we don't want to hurt you," the big man with red hair yells out.

Really? It sure looks like you are trying to do just that.

"Just lay face down on the mattress with your hands behind your back."

Okay fine. Do your magic. Give me the shots. Take me to the psychiatrist again. I don't care anymore. I want him gone. Make him get out of my head. "Please make him stop." I lay down on the mattress face down. I've done this enough times to know the drill.

Pieces of green beans squish against my face. I'm vile. I'm hopeless. I just want it to stop.

The cell door unlocks and slides open. The men enter my room one by one. The handcuffs slap tightly on my wrists. I'm lifted up by force. My arms stretch back behind me.

"We're going to medical again Gavin."

Yeah, no shit. It's the only way. I'm getting what I deserve. The guards stand me up. Mashed potatoes squish between my toes. I can't do this anymore. I can't keep him inside.

9

"Let's go sir." I'm led down the dark and dingy hall towards medical. This is the walk of shame. Monica stares at me with fright in her eyes. We were just joking about a beer. What happened? The rage. I can't control it. I can't keep it in anymore. My brain is exploding with urges. Who is this? A man's body is lifeless on the floor in his cell. His clothing is soaked, grass is everywhere. We walk by his head. It's Andrew. Oh Andrew. You will learn.

We are not allowed to act out in here. Not even a little bit. We are treated like animals but we can't turn into one. The moment we let out the real us, they cannot handle it. I can handle it Andrew. You can show your true self to me. I will understand.

"Stop staring and start moving sir." The guards yank on my arms. Why not just put a collar on my neck and pull me with a leash? Next comes the pills. The voices. The hallucinations. These people don't know me. They don't know what they are doing.

I walk the walk of shame to medical. They think they can just drug the monster inside me. But they can't. I've tried. Countless nights of drinking never took it away. I can't be tamed. I need blood and flesh. No pill or injection will ever change it. Please just destroy me. I can't take it anymore. The compulsion. The rage. The monster. He knows me. He tells me what to do. If I feed him, he goes away. I pay him with flesh. Once my alter of skulls was complete, he was going to go away. It was promised.

No one will ever understand. The torture. The control.

"Pick up the pace Gavin. You gotta see the doctor."

I move my bare feet faster. The food is still caked in between my toes. There is dirt sticking to the food. Andrew will understand. I saw it in his eyes. He's genuine. There aren't many people like him. We will meet somehow. I just have to clean up my act. I need one person to understand. I want someone to meet the monster within. The only people that met the monster are dead. They gave their life to subdue him.

Episode 3

"Hello? Elizabeth?"

My voice is raspy. My body feels numb. Everything hurts. Where am I? Where is Elizabeth? Did I complete the mission? "Pumpkin? Two Teethers?"

Where is everyone? My clothes feel wet against my skin. I can taste the faint flavor of a menthol cigarette. My mind fades to the last thing I remember, the yard. Right. They tried. They were going to take me. But it wasn't time yet. There is more to do. I grunt as I roll onto my side. I was drooling on the dirt caked floor.

"Well hello cutie pie." Elizabeth? She's here? She can't be here.

"You've been out for quite some time; I have some food for you."

I grunt loudly and roll to face the front of my cell. I see a disappointing sight. It's not Elizabeth. She has a nice smile though.

"I also have your pills. It's a nice cocktail for you."

It's a sign. I am getting ready. I need to become stronger. The pills will alter my body just enough to survive in the portal. Then I will have exactly five hours. I will face a room of thirty of them. They are coming from different realms.

They will receive the word. Let's hope I can deliver it well. I attended the seminary for a reason. I was teaching everyone The Word of God within a week after attending. I was the best student they had. No wonder I was chosen for this mission.

I bend my leg and prop up on one knee. My body has never ached this bad before. My head is pounding. I'm dizzy.

"I'm going to slide your tray through sir." The woman reminds me of a waitress at my local diner. The Country Inn. I can trust her. Is she aware of the mission? She must be.

2

"Thank you, ma'am. How long until the pills start to take effect?"

"It depends Andrew. Everyone is different. You may feel a little drowsy. Your mouth might get a little dry. I'll give you extra water." Everyone? So, these have been tested. That's good.

"Has anyone else gone through the portal?" The dark-haired woman lets out a wild laugh.

"Just me Andrew. I go through the portal a lot." She continues to laugh. I kneel in front of the cell door and take my tray of food. It's chicken with gravy and vegetables. On the side is a biscuit and some juice. In a small compartment in the tray are pills.

There is a large white pill, two small blue ones and a red and yellow capsulated one. The food isn't what Ma would make but it'll do for now.

"My name is Monica by the way."

"Thank you, Ma'am."

"Don't call me Ma'am, that makes me sound old." Monica is smiling from ear to ear. It feels nice to see a friendly face. I wish it were Elizabeth and the girls though. But this is my mission. I have to do this alone.

3

"Where are you from Mr. Clark?" She's prying. Is she a spy? It seems too good to be true that someone wants to get to know me.

"Small-town, U.S.A.," I reply slyly to Monica. Monica let's out another wild laugh.

"I will be right back," she exclaims mid laugh. Monica turns and heads down the cement hallway. She is wearing gray slacks and a tight black shirt. She isn't thin but she isn't fat by no means. I can hear her heels clanking against the floor. The sound becomes fainter as she heads down the hall.

I'm left with my tray and my own company. I bring my tray over to the cement bed. No pillow or blanket. Not even a Bible. This isn't exactly a hotel. However, I wouldn't even treat an animal this way. Or an enemy. I wince as I sit down onto the cold cement. My pants are stuck to my skin. Do I take the pills before or after the food?

If I take the pills first, they will be more potent. The stronger I get, the faster we can get through this mission. Is the yellow and red pill a pain pill? I hope so. I put all of the pills in my hand and dump them into my mouth.

4

"So, what was the outburst for Gavin? I don't understand. You were doing so good." Like he would understand. He doesn't know what the hell I go through. I am so sick of this charade. If I have to come see this whack job one more time, I'm going to explode. What's my excuse this time? Why can't they just let me be?

"I need a drink doc." It's all I can manage. I need a drink of blood but I will settle for a brewsky.

"Gavin, you know that's not going to happen. Just put those thoughts out of your mind. Drinking alcohol is not going save you." Yeah, no shit doc. You guys took everything from me. I had it all. And now it's gone.

"You don't know how hard it is, you get to leave this place. You can eat whatever you want." Whoever you want. "Stop it! Goddammit, shut the fuck up!" I jump up but my legs are chained to the bottom of the chair. "Fuck! Just make it stop! I'll do anything!"

"Gavin! Gavin!" The doctor is yelling in my face but I only hear a faint sound. He can't stop it. No one can. I need about five shots of hard liquor and a six pack to make it stop. Even though it's only momentarily. Until I come to with a knife in my hand. Then it's out of my control. It wasn't their fault. It wasn't my fault. It's the voices. "Make it stop! Make it stop!"

5

"Hey there handsome." It's Monica. She walks up with a gray metal gold up chair. It looks very familiar. I've only unfolded thousands of them. Life as a custodian isn't easy but it has its perks. I get paid time off, weekends off, plus overtime. It puts food on the table for the girls. I dip the biscuit into the gravy and take a huge bite.

My Ma would have put this cook to shame. I would give anything to have her cooking one more time. I miss her and my Pa so much. I have no one, except for Elizabeth and the girls. I stare at Monica blankly with my mouth full of food. Not to be rude, but I'm starving.

Monica is holding a clipboard and a pen. She is slowly moving her pen across a paper. Who does she report to? "Andrew, are you hearing voices?" I swallow my food hard. She knows too much. Did they tell her? Can she hear my thoughts right now?

"Monica, where are you from?" She lets out a huge smile.

"Well that's a first, typically I'm the one asking all of the questions. I knew there was something special about you Andrew. Let's just say I'm from Big City, U.S.A." I let out a laugh straight from my belly. She tagged me back alright.

6

"I see you have a wedding ring on, who's the lucky lady?" Monica winks at me.

"Her name is Elizabeth." Elizabeth wouldn't understand any of this. She is just going to have to wait and see. I am going to save us all. Once I deliver my message, everything will be fine.

"Do you want me to get ahold of her for you?" She can't come here! She will blow this thing wide open. Plus, she could get hurt. Her role is to be with the girls. This mission is too dangerous. It's our fault. All of the sinning we do. The members of the other realms of the

universe were shocked when they saw how we
conduct ourselves.

"After my meeting, I will call her. I have
to make sure it's safe." Surely Monica is aware
of what is going on. It's obvious they sent her in
here to soften me up.

Monica let's out one of her wild laughs.
She is such a good actress. She's pretending that
she has no idea what is going on in this place.
My mind is swirling. My mouth feels dry.
What's happening to me? Monica's face gets
blurry.

7

"Whatever you say Mr. Clark. I'm sure
your wife would love to speak with you."
Monica stands up and picks up her chair and
walks away. The heels of her shoes echo down

the long dusty hallway. Where is she going? Surely, she has to warn the others. The pills are working their magic.

Surely, I will wake up a new man. I will be stronger and faster. No one will be able to stop me! My mouth is too dry to finish my food. I get up with my tray. I'm trying to walk but I'm stumbling. I bend down and set my food in the corner of my cell. I stumble back to the cement bed and plop down feeling heavy. Damn those pills hit me hard.

I'm starting to feel nauseous. I can't get sick though. I will blow this whole mission. The pills have to take effect. I wouldn't mind a pillow or even a blanket. I must be strong though. I am being tested.

8

The walls of my cell are spinning. I'm not going to make it am I? I am just a pawn, aren't I? They are testing the pills to make sure they are safe. I lean back against the cold, damp wall. The cement is hard on the back of my head.

"Daddy, make the igloo higher." I rolled the snowball through the yard. Two Teethers always thought I was so strong. My wife and children and I always had fun together. Our house is our own little slice of heaven. I can hear the laughter of the girls from that cold winter day. It's like I'm lying in the snow right now.

Dana ran through the yard in purple snow pants and Carrie had on pink ones. Those girls mean everything to me. The girls laughed with excitement as their big strong Daddy rolled the snowball through the yard. Pieces of leaves and grass got stuck to the snow in my hands.

I picked up the snowball in my hands. I held it over my head and let out a big roar and started chasing the girls. Their screams pierced through the crisp cold air.

9

"Stop it Andrew, you're scaring them." Elizabeth was always the voice of reason. She made sure that there was balance.

"They're fine dear, they love it." Those girls deserve the world. Daddy is going to make it right, I promise. I took the snowball and stacked it on the others.

We built a huge igloo. We did good. Amazing things happen when people work together. All we have is our family. Everyone else are just strangers. These people don't know me. They don't know the real me. But Elizabeth and the girls understand. They know the real me.

The back of my head melts into the cement wall. A bright green light appears on the cement wall in front of me. It's glowing from the moisture in the wall. A red and black bloody hand comes through. It's headed towards my face.

My mouth is too dry to scream. I can't even swallow. "Andrew, it's almost time," a raspy voice comes from the wall. My eyes are so heavy. I'm forcing them open. I'm helpless. My legs are numb.

All I can hear is a faint dripping of water in the corner. Then I see him.

"Hello Andrew, I'm starving, can I join you?" He's thin. He has on thick glasses with a wire frame. Is this who I'm supposed to meet with? Who is he? Where did he come from? My tongue is completely dry. I can no longer speak or swallow.

"I'm Gavin, nice to meet you."

Amy Perez MS Psychology

Episode 4

1

"Keep it moving Gavin." Of course. I can't have an interaction in here. The guard holds my handcuffs tight. It's hard to shuffle my feet with these chains. Where is my Father right now? My Grandma? Do they care that I'm here? Are they going to come here? Surely, they will have something to say about what I've done. You will rot for this.

"Shut up! Shut the fuck up! Stop talking to me." I jerk as hard as I can. Make it stop!

"Yo calm down!" The guard is screaming in my face. "Do you need to go back to medical?" His red hair gleams in the dusty light of the hallway. His green eyes are piercing right through me.

"I need a damn beer." It would help for now.

"Don't we all." The cell doors slam behind me.

"Aren't you going to take off my cuffs?" Great. Last time this happened it took hours to get a guard in here. "Thanks!" I am yelling to no one. They don't hear me. No one does. I slump down against the bars of my cell. My eyes are burning. What time is it? How long was I with the doc? I've stayed up all night ever since I was a child. The night calls to me. So did the animals. They didn't stand a chance against my strength and knife.

My Father was pissed when he found that rabbit behind the house. Only he didn't know it wasn't my first kill. It definitely wasn't my last. He made me promise I would stop. "Gavin this can't go on. This is isn't normal. Just be like the other boys." But I tried. When I saw the other boys play baseball, the joy on their face when they hit the ball looked familiar. It was the same joy I felt when I would feel warm blood on my skin.

"Hi Gavin."

"Holy shit, you scared me." I was so lost in thought; I didn't hear her walk up.

"How are you feeling today Gavin?"

I'm better now Monica, I'm sorry about the other day. Monica, there is no getting well from this.

2

It's a new day. My mind feels clear. We just need to do something about these dirty floors. Maybe I can get a cigarette from the boss man. How did I get here? I remember fighting with Elizabeth. Why was I so angry? Damn I upset the girls, didn't I? I need to call Elizabeth. I stand up from the concrete. I feel rested. My eyes feel slightly fuzzy but my mind feels so clear. I walk over to the front of my cell and look both ways down the long hallway.

It's a ghost town in here. All I can hear is the water dripping in the corner of my cell. I walk over to the toilet and peer inside. The brown water looks back at me. I pull down my orange pants to use the bathroom. I hear heels clanking down the hall. Never mind. I pull my pants back up as fast as I can. It's her. I vaguely remember her. Big city woman.

"Andrew! How are you feeling?" The dark-haired woman yells down the hall.

"I'm good Miss."

The woman's heels pick up the pace.

"Stay put, let me go grab a chair."

Young lady, I'm not going anywhere. I could use a fresh shower and shave. Also, a smoke and some coffee. A fast food breakfast sandwich and I'd be good to go. I gotta get back to work. Elizabeth and the girls need me. How did I get here? How long did I sleep for? I walk up and grab the bars. They are cold and coarse. My saliva feels sticky in my mouth. Maybe this young lady can get me a toothbrush. Maybe she has the keys to this cell.

3

"Hey there handsome!" I'm met with a big smile and some pills. "Do you remember me?"

"Big city girl." I typically don't forget names but her name is slipping my mind.

"Or you can call me Monica. I am the nurse for this unit."

"Thanks Monica, did you come to break me out of here?" Monica let's out a wild laugh. I remember her laugh now.

"Have you had any strange thoughts about portals or are you hearing any voices?" Monica's tone turned to serious.

Strange question. I'm feeling puzzled. Is this woman drunk? She must be testing me. Just remain calm. Don't get upset.

"No Ma'am."

Monica sits down and starts marking her paper. "Andrew, do you know why you are here?"

"Honestly, I don't. I'm thinking clear but my memory feels poor. The last thing I remember is getting in a fight with my wife."

"Andrew, we have diagnosed you with paranoid schizophrenia."

Now I'm the one who feels like laughing. "What?"

"Paranoid schizophrenia." Monica is talking but I just hear a faint humming sound. What does this mean for me? Am I staying in here? Is this a life sentence. Confusion washes over me. Do I need to prove my innocence now? What do these people want from me?

"Once you take your meds, shower and eat, you will meet with Doctor Chadwick. He will go over everything with you."

"Yes Ma'am." Monica looks at me playfully. "Don't say Ma'am it makes me feel old."

"Sorry about that, I'm from the South so that's just how we talk."

"I thought you had a bit of an accent. I wasn't sure though. I have your meds right here." Monica hands me two Styrofoam cups through the cell bars. One is half full of pills. The other is halfway full of orange juice.

"Take those and the guards will take you out for a shower and some time outside." Monica takes her clipboard and chair and heads down the hall. What were those big words she was using? Surely this is a mistake. I peer down in my cups. Good Lord, that's a lot of pills. What is the point of this? I take a sip of the orange juice. One by one I take the pills. "Yo boss man." A familiar voice booms down the hall. It's the man with the lighter.

"Hey boss, how's it goin?" A pill is half stuck in my throat. I don't wanna miss my chance to get a smoke.

"I'm good man, are you ready for a shower?" James has a handful of clothes and a bar of soap.

"Does it come with a smoke?"

James parts his lips to show his gapped teeth. I remember being out in the yard. It was raining. Who was I yelling at?

4

"Sure thing Mr. Clark." James unlocks my cell and I step through cautiously. The boss leans down and shackles my ankles. I follow him shuffling down the hall.

"Hello Andrew."

I look over to my right. What the? How does this man know my name? He's standing against the cell tapping his fingers as if he's playing a flute. Am I supposed to know him? "Fine morning huh?"

"That's enough Gavin." James shoots the man a look. Gavin. Doesn't sound familiar. "Don't lose your chance Gavin, you get out of seg today."

"That's right." The man shoots me a Hollywood smile. What is seg? I'm so confused. I need to speak to Elizabeth. We enter into a shower area.

"Take your time Mr. Clark. You are meeting the doctor later and a lawyer too." I look at James with wide eyes. A lawyer? A doctor? This ain't good. I step inside the shower with my shackled ankles. This seems like a good time to pray. God, can you bring me some light. Show me a sign that you are there. I need some guidance. I turn the shower to hot. My mouth is so dry. I put my mouth under the beams of water to take a drink. Warm beads of water hit the back of my throat.

"Carrie."

"What Elizabeth?" I looked at her with sleepy eyes.

"Let's name her Carrie." My pregnant wife had a wide smile on her face. I had fallen asleep during the movie. I reached around and rested my hand on her belly. "I like Norma, after my Grandmother too though." I wanted Elizabeth to have her way though. She has to go through the labor. Thank god men aren't in charge of havin' the babies. Our population would be slim. I ain't pushin' no bowling ball outta me. Elizabeth is a tough woman. She begged me for one more baby.

I rub the bar of soap in my hands and then scrub my hair and face. "Five minutes Mr. Clark." Right, I forgot where I was for a minute.

5

I rinse off my face and hair and turn the water off. The water stops for a moment and then thick rusty orange water spits out all over my chest. Great. I take the dingy towel and dry off. I wish I could take these chains off. How do I get out of here? What is the doctor going to say? "Yo, I got you a smoke Mr. Clark." Yes!

"Any hot coffee with that?"

"They got decaf in the cafeteria; I can see what I can do." Well it's better than nothin'. I heard even decaf has a faint amount of caffeine.

"Right this way Mr. Clark." Into the changing cell. I lean down to dry my legs. The chains are dripping with water. James unlocks the chains and grasps them in his hands and leaves the cell.

"Let me run to the cafeteria sir, lemme check on the coffee situation."

Hell yeah, I'm startin' to feel like a brand-new man. I slide a pair of white briefs on. I dry my hair with the towel. I reach around my back with the towel and rub it back on forth. Ah, brand new. I'm ready to get back to work now. I just need my work shirt, some jeans and a mop and I'm ready to go. Shit. The mission. What am I doing? "The doctor" and "the lawyer". I better get my shit together. Today is the day. I need a bible by my side.

"Alright let's go." James has a steaming cup of coffee and a nice smoke in his hand. Good, I need it. I need to prepare.

"Good news boss, no more shackles. Monica vouched for you. So, don't let her down."

"I sure won't, I gotta show them that I'm good, I'm gonna prove it for all of us. People are inherently good."

"Sure, thing boss, you got it." I follow James to the red door. It's the portal. The meeting. Here goes nothin'. The autumn air hits my damp face. The cement is cold beneath my bare feet. I'm free! No chains, no shackles. I'm free to complete the mission.

"Here you go Andrew." James hands me the smoke and coffee. I like cream and sugar but black will do. Like clockwork a lighter is lit in front of my face. I suck the smoke into my mouth. I don't inhale though. No way. I slowly exhale the smoke. "That'll work boss, thank you." James gives me an approving nod and a slight smile. Then I see him, the doctor.

6

We're surrounded. The barbed wire fence is protecting us from infiltration. Beyond that orange, red and yellow trees are keeping us out of sight. My feet brush through the wet grass towards a single bench. Sitting on the top is the doctor. I can tell. It's him. It's time. "Yo doc!" I yell out as I pick up the pace. He slightly turns his hard to reveal a sneaky smile. Shit. That's no doctor, this whole thing is a set up. I recognize him from the cell.

"No doc here, just a man wanting a cold one."

"That stuff ain't no good man believe me. I watched my Pa go down that road."

"Oh yeah, did that road lead him in a place like this? Names Gavin." The man holds out a hand from atop a damp wooden picnic table. I set down my coffee and shake his hand. His hands are thin and bony. He's shaking.

"Andrew, Andrew Clark." Something isn't right. "You're not the doctor?"

"No sir, I'm stuck in this place just like you. You will meet the doctor though. He's got enough pills to make you sleep for days." I'm not sure if I want that.

"I take it you aren't a lawyer either?" The thin man lets out a laugh.

"You are in the right place Andrew. I'm not a damn lawyer that's for sure. Thanks for the vote of confidence though."

Who is this man? Why are we here together? I take a long drag off my smoke. A long piece of ash collected at the end. My mouth fills with smoke as I ash my cigarette into the grass. Oh. Oh, how could I be so stupid? This is the meeting. He is from another realm. I'm supposed to be preaching. I need to prove that we are good. "Do you know what heaven looks like Gavin?"

7

"I think I'm getting an idea. Are you a holy man?"

"Yes, yes I am, I stammer out." I'm so nervous, I can't blow this, the world is depending on me. Not to mention my little girls. "I went to a college to study the bible."

"Oh, is that right? And what kind of bullshit did they jam down your throat?" Gavin let's out a loud sigh. "Sorry man, we're not on the same page. Enjoy your smoke." Gavin slips his sandals on and gets up off the bench.

"There's gold!" I manage.

"Gold? Where?" Gavin gives me a snide look.

"The roads, they are made of gold, and you sit on golden benches. And you can have anything you want!"

"Look man, I don't know what kind of shit you are on, but you need to chill out." James comes strolling through the grass.

"We alright boys? You two both get a chance to get out of segregation, so don't screw it up."

"We're good boss, I was just telling Gavin about heaven." Gavin's eyes light up. I've gotten his attention now. Thank God, literally. I just need him to report back to his people. I have my work cut out for me. Good thing I'm a hard worker.

"Aight, keep it clean out here, a few more minutes gentlemen." James walks away whistling. He sure is a nice man.

"Heaven?" Gavin asks.

"Yes sir, that's heaven," I tell him. It's the truth.

"Even for me?"

"Especially for you." I gotta explain everything as simple as possible. This man doesn't know about God. It's obvious.

8

"You really have lost it, nice talking to you." Gavin walks through the grass.

Shit! I blew it. Gold? Really? What was I thinking? I mean that's how I picture it. What else was I supposed to say? I need another chance. I turn to run after him but he's gone. Where did he go? Did I just imagine that? Was he real? Was that just a practice round? James gives me a gapped smile.

"Couple more minute's boss man," he yells out across the yard.

"Sure thing," I yell back. I take a seat on top of the bench. I must save us all. I have to. I look up at the sky. It's gray. A small amount of sunlight shines through. Typical fall sky. I take a long hit off of my cigarette. It's about at the filter. My mouth fills with smoke. I hold it there for a moment. I should have gone with a different angle. But how do you preach the bible to someone from another planet? Gotta keep it simple.

"Go to sleep Andrew." My Ma tucked me into my small bed. She pulled the thin flannel blanket up to my chin. "I love you." My Ma kissed my forehead. "I know, I love you too." I closed my eyes as my Ma began to sing. I never told her but she wasn't the best of singers. I loved it anyway. I would pretend to be asleep to save her. I knew she had to get to work. She worked nights at our local grocery store. My Pa was so busy drinking up all of his money. Even still, he had a special treat just for me. After a long night of drinking, he would bring me a bag of potato chips, a Hershey bar and a glass bottle of Coca Cola. It was the best. I always looked forward to my treat.

"Let's go Mr. Clark." Right. Gotta go. I put my cigarette out in the wet grass and take it with me. I don't wanna leave a mess out here. I walk across the grass toward James. He's waiting to take me where I need to go.

"Where to now boss?"

"Well, you get to eat breakfast in the cafeteria."

"Oh really?"

"You got it." James whips open the door.

I'm ready for some dippin' eggs, sausage and grits for sure. That'll do me. And some of Ma's biscuits and gravy.

"Oh, your wife called too boss."

Elizabeth, I'm gonna fix this. I'm gonna make it right. I just gotta find Gavin.

Amy Perez MS Psychology

Episode 5

1

I don't need this place. This prison. I'm already a prisoner in my own brain. I can't tell anyone my deepest darkest thoughts. Hell, I can't even scratch the surface. Nice to meet you. I'm fantasizing about eating your heart out. Not exactly the way to start out.

Just make it go away! I need a different mind. Or some shots. These demons need to go to sleep. I stare down at the sorry excuse for a breakfast. I thought diner food was bad. Why is there water surrounding these scrambled eggs? Also, this watered-down decaf has to go. "Sit down Gavin!"

The anger on my Grandma's face is still fresh in my mind. "What is this Gavin? What in the hell is this?" She had a bloody pocket knife in her hand. I knew her vision wasn't the greatest. I was scared to see what she was going to say about the dried blood.

"You can't just leave this stuff lying around your room." She was so angry. She was putting my laundry away and almost sliced her hand open. She didn't know that I used it on my victim. I left the blood on the knife as a trophy. How could I be so careless? So stupid. Only hours before, the blade sunk into Ken's abdomen.

2

I savored every moment. We were dating for only a couple of weeks. I couldn't hold back any longer. The voices were too loud. There was only one way to silence them. It had to be done.

It had to be Ken. Was it out of opportunity? I enjoyed my time with him. I enjoyed the sex. Even though I wasn't supposed to feel that way. My Grandma was constantly asking about girlfriends. Fuck that. What is wrong with me?

Why can't I just be normal? I fucked everything up. I pick up a slightly rusted fork and hold it up. I need to get rid of them. The demons. They are haunting me.

Why can't my Grandma understand? Girls are not my style. Hell, even living humans are not my style. I can only make it so far. I have to taste the blood. It's like I don't have control. I have this fork. How far can I get with it? "Hey boss. Got room for one more?"

3

I stab my jagged fork into the crusty biscuit. It breaks in half.

"Fuck!"

"Set your mind on things above, not earthly things."

"What are you talking about Andrew?"

"It's from the bible, I want to bring you the word."

Is this guy serious? "The word?"

"Yes, we as humans are good people. Deep down, we are all good. I can prove it to you."

Bullshit. Look buddy. You don't know me. You have no idea why I am here do you? Haven't you seen the news? Did you just crawl out from under a rock? I finally got out of solitude I'm not going to last long in here.

My face is splashed all over the news. I am a notorious serial killer Andrew. We are not all good. But let's see where this goes?

"Oh yeah? Even me?"

"Of course, even you. We are all God's children."

I let out a wicked laugh. I expose dried biscuit in my mouth as I cover my laughter with my hand. This guy has lost his mind.

"What did they get you for Andrew?"

"The nurse gave me a long word. Something that starts with an S."

That's it huh? A diagnosis? Not everyone is one hundred percent honest in this place. You never want to give yourself away. The less people know, the better.

4

"I will go see the doctor today."

"Good 'ole Doctor Chadwick huh?" Doctor fucking Chadwick. He's full of pills, needles and inhumane treatment. Don't expect much help from him. If anything, he makes matters worse.

"Well hopefully he can fix you up. This isn't a place for a guy like you."

Andrew doesn't speak though. His eyes are open wide. He's staring off into space with a goofy smile on his face.

"Hello? Earth to Andrew." Where did he go? Maybe he's taking that religious shit too far.

I pick up an orange slice and sink my teeth into the pulp. It's as close to skin as I'm going to get.

5

"Andrew? What's wrong with you?" Nothing. How does someone just space out like that? So weird. I take a sip of watered-down coffee. It tastes more like black tea. I gag a little from the taste.

"Gavin, I am a Christian woman. I don't want to go to Hell for your sins." I had never seen my Grandma so mad. If she was that angry over a knife, what would she think about what I did with knife? Ken was buried feet away in the backyard.

She had no idea I dismembered him in her basement. That was only a small knife I used to start the process.

Thankfully, she didn't find the rest of my "supplies". What's this asshole looking at? Head shaved. Full of tattoos. His eyes are literally burning through me.

6

I glance at him and quickly dart me eyes away. He must recognize me. I don't know how long I've been in here. Who knows when he got here. They don't exactly keep us up to date with current events in here. They want us to be confused. They capitalize on experimenting on us.

Dr. Chadwick doesn't know what to do with us.

"He's catatonic." Monica's voice cuts through my thoughts. I didn't even notice her walk up. She shines a light in Andrews eyes.

"Andrew?"

Wow I have never seen anything like that before. What is this place? Surely, I'm in a prison. A lot of people in here are not like me. It's like they are out of it. Or do I look like that too?

"Call the President Goddammit! Only he knows about it!" The man with the tattoos jumps up on top of the chair.

"Call him! Call him!"

7

"Thomas! Get down!" Monica yells across the dingy cafeteria. I am suddenly missing my cell. Does that guy really think he can just call the president? I take a closer look around me. There are some men with hospital gowns on and others in prison clothes.

I look up and down the walls. At the top of the walls there are broken windows. It's too high to climb out. This isn't just a plain prison. Not that I would know, this is my first time in one. I glance over at Monica. She's taking Andrew's vitals.

Two large men dressed in hospital scrubs come in with a wheelchair. They look like they are in the middle of a battlefield. Wide eyed and moving fast.

"One, two, three." Simultaneously they lift Andrew onto the wheelchair. They wheel him off as Monica trails behind them. What in the hell happened to Andrew?

8

"Do you know where you are?"

I see him but I can't speak. My mouth is dry. Who is this man? How did I get here? His face is so close to mine. I can smell his breath. I see oily white hair met with a wrinkled face.

"Andrew? Hello?"

Hello. Yes. I'm here. How can I help you?

"H…h…hello." I manage to stammer out. Why is it so difficult to speak? What happened? Where am I?

"Hello Andrew, I'm Dr. Chadwick. I know you have met Monica."

I glance over at a concerned face. Big city girl. Of course. My brain feels fuzzy. I feel like I'm in a fog. I have a strong craving for a cigarette and I need a bottle of Coca Cola.

"Andrew, do you know why you are here?"

The man is talking very slow and loudly. I've never been spoken like this before. What is wrong with him?

"Andrew?"

"Y…y…ess?"

"Andrew, we have diagnosed you with paranoid schizophrenia."

Paranoid what? It's the S word again. Maybe they can write that down for me. What day is it? What time is it? I need to get to work. I got bills to pay.

"You are losing touch with reality Andrew."

Well of course doc, look at this place. This isn't supposed to be my reality. I'm just a custodian from a small town. I'm a husband and a father.

"I'm a good man," I manage.

9

"Andrew, I don't deny that but we need to get you out of this psychosis. It's going to take a lot of medicinal therapy to correct you. If we can."

My ears are ringing. If we can? What the hell does that mean? What is he talking about?

"We have begun treatment but it could take a while for the effects to take place."

This can't be happening. I need to get out of here.

"Clozapine, zotepine and lithium."

"Doc, I'm confused."

"Confusion is normal. We will work hard to get you better. We need you to take an injection and head back to your cell."

Monica approaches with a tray of pills and a syringe full of clear liquid. A guard slaps chains around my ankles before I can even react. Two men hold my arms down as I try and break free.

"I need to talk to Elizabeth!"

"Andrew calm down. We can do this the calm way or the not so calm way, you decide."

Monica's voice soothes my beating heart only slightly. This is not a calm situation. Then I feel the pain from the needle.

Schizophrenic Episode Series

Episode 6

1

Shit. It's freezing in here. "Have I landed?" I don't remember leaving. "We are good people I promise." Can they hear me? There must be over three hundred of them. "There is no need to send anyone else through the portal." I barely made it through alive myself. My teeth are chattering so hard I can barely speak.

My skin feels sticky. Are they ready to hear The Word? I have the entire bible memorized. I was made for this mission. The earth depends on me. These creatures don't look to friendly. Many of them have multiple heads and eyes. I have to stop them.

"The Lord knows the way of the righteous, but the way of the wicked will perish." Hopefully that is a good place to start.

"Wait! Where is everyone going? What did I say?"

One by one, the figures fade into darkness. I blew it. How could I let that happen?

"Come back!" It's too late. That was my only chance. I needed to grab their attention. I was almost certain that was a great place to start.

"Do not be afraid for I am with you!" I shout to no one. I'm angry but I can't move my body. My heart is pumping so hard that it might explode. Blood is surging in my fingertips and toes. All of that studying for nothing. No one knows the bible better than me.

"Hello Andrew."

They came back? I can't see anyone. My vision is blurred. My eyes feel thick and heavy. My brain is swirling and so is my stomach. Are more people coming through the portal? Dear God I hope not. They won't survive. I'm barely holding on by a thread.

"Andrew, you're shaking!"

"Elizabeth? Carrie? Dana?" Is my family here? Please don't harm my girls.

"I need medical!"

I hear a clicking sound. I've heard it before. Big city girl. Her shoes. She has come for me.

"Come quick." I hear a faint voice in the background.

"Yes! I need you!" Fast hard clicks come closer.

"Andrew?"

I try to move my legs but they are chained together.

"Hello?"

"Andrew, it's Monica, can you hear me?"

2

"Monica, I blew it."

"Blew what Andrew?" Monica sounds alarmed.

"I had my chance. I gave them The Word and they vanished."

I hear men murmuring.

"Yes, he's in a psychosis."

My cell door creaks open.

"Goddammit, help him!" Monica is panicking.

"Do your job for once!"

"We already gave him an injection," a man's voice shouts out.

Please no. I can't survive anything else. My body hurts so bad. Every muscle is stiff. The back of my eyes are burning.

"Do not be afraid for I am with you," I manage to stammer. It's all I have left in case they can still hear me. Only they can stop this. They need to show me some mercy.

"How long has he been awake for?"

"Not long."

A bony hand touches my sweat filled forehead.

"Andrew, it's Doctor Chadwick."

"Doc, I need a smoke and some air." I can't breathe. Internally, I'm panicking but my body is paralyzed.

"You heard him Monica! Why are you just standing there?"

Fast clicks beat down the cement.

"Doc, the portal." He needs to know. "I barely made it; they can't survive."

"What portal Andrew?"

So, he's just going to act like he doesn't know? I've been set up. We are being recorded. "Doc, don't play with me."

"Just hang in there Andrew."

"I told you, you put too much." Another man's voice is coming closer.

"Who is the damn doctor? Not you!" He's angry and authoritative. "Monica is getting him a smoke."

"Well that's the least you could do."

Who is that? I don't recognize his voice. I roll slowly over to my back. One by one, each area of my spine cracks into place. I look up at an old, dirty cement ceiling. I hear clicks from a pair of heels coming closer.

"Yo boss how you doin'?" A man with a gapped smile is standing over me. He has a cigarette and a lighter in his hand. I roll onto my elbow. The room starts to spin. I feel awful.

"Yo man he looks bad."

"Just light the cigarette," the doc snaps at my friend from Alabama. If my strength was up, I would smack him one. You don't talk to people like that. I don't care who you are. James looks at me with concern.

"You alright boss." His compassion surprises me. James is holding a menthol one hundred and a lighter in his hand. He holds the cigarette towards my lips. His hand is shaking. He's frightened. Does he know I failed my mission? How much time do we have left? They are going to destroy us. I feel a soft cigarette filter touch my lips. The sound of a spark from a lighter hits my ears. A flame heats up under my nose.

3

Out of reflex, I breath in the smoke of the menthol. It feels like heaven in my mouth. I reach up and grab my smoke. I'm weak but I ain't that weak. I'm a big strong man dammit. If I didn't think these people were trying to help me, I could run through them and escape this fortress.

But I must complete this. I exhale a big cloud of smoke.

"You good man?" James is very concerned. He takes a seat on my cement bed. He leaves his legs open and rests his elbows on his thighs.

"Oh yeah boss," I say mid cough. My throat feels dry but the cigarette is waking up my brain. I needed that. I'm awake now. I can hear arguing voices down the hall.

"You can't give him any more shots!" Monica screams. Then I hear heeled clicks coming towards my cell. I cling to the cigarette between my fingers. I bring my smoke up to my mouth again. I take a big drag. I'm contemplating inhaling. I'm starting to feel like myself again. Please no more shots. The last one nearly killed me. I pray that no one else has to go through that. What in the hell was the liquid in that thing? Liquid death.

I slowly sit up being careful not to drop my menthol. My butt and legs hurt so bad. I've felt better after working eighteen hours straight. What did they put me through? I look down at the floor. It's damp and covered with dirt. My toenails are black. I feel like a piece of garbage. There is even dirt in my leg hair. When was the last time I showered or even used the bathroom?

"You were out like a light man." James looks at me empathetically.

"Oh yeah?"

"Yeah man, every time I walked by your cell, you were out cold. I don't know why they did that to you but it ain't right."

"The last thing I remember was them telling me I had paranoid something."

James looks at me wide-eyed.

"Schizophrenia?"

"Yeah that's the word."

James let's out a laugh. "Shit man, you ain't schizophrenic man."

I look at him confused.

"I done seen schizophrenic and you ain't it."

The confusion sets in. Who do I listen to? Who do I trust?

4

"You can go now James. The showers and the yard need to get tended to."

James let's out a big sigh.

"You ain't schizo man. Don't let them fool you."

"That's enough James, you can go." Monica is stern and direct. I look down at my cigarette. A large ash has collected at the end. Typically, I would use an ashtray. At this moment, I don't think it matters. I lightly ash next to me. James walks out of my cell and down the long hallway. I can hear the scuffs getting more faint.

"I'm glad you're okay." Monica rests her hand on my shoulder. She has manicured nails with red polish. I can smell her perfume. The scent is familiar. Lavender.

"Let me get some food and coffee."

"Thank you," I choke through my smoke.

"First, we'll get you cleaned up Andrew."

I nod my head to agree.

"That'll work."

I'm ready to get out of here. I need to get on the phone. I gotta call Elizabeth, Anthony and my job. In that order. I take another drag off my smoke. I'm coming back from the dead. Hopefully the experimenting is over.

I can't survive that one again. I can't believe I'm in this place. I need to apologize to Elizabeth. Why were we fighting again? Oh yeah, those damn animals. We are gonna have to come to an agreement. One or two pets is fine, but she is taking it too far. I work too damn hard to watch a bunch of animals destroy my house. I take another puff. I'm ready to get the hell out of here.

I've done everything I can do. I'm done with these people. James is the only person in here who shows some respect. He's a good man. He should be in charge. I get up slowly and shuffle to the toilet and drop my lit cigarette inside. I don't know when the next time I'll get a smoke will be.

5

"Thanks Andrew." My supervisor gave me a huge smile and a gift card to our local grocery store.

"Thanks sir." I was happy to do my job. But I was happier to see the smiling face outside my boss's door. It was little Pumpkin. She loved coming to work with me. I can see her blonde hair and blue eyes right now. I could never do anything wrong in her eyes. It's so hard to make time for work and play. She loves coming to work with her Dad. I think her favorite part is the cookie and chocolate milk at the end of our shift. And of course, the basketball. Her Dad is good at shootin' hoops. My little Pumpkin. Daddy will be home soon sweetheart. I promise.

This is all a misunderstanding. I was never supposed to end up in here. It wasn't supposed to be this way. I wish Carrie and I were together right now. We could be walking down our favorite dirt trail. We love looking at the nature. I could be pushing the girls on their swing right now. I'm sorry girls. Daddy is gonna fix this.

"Yo boss, let's get you cleaned up. Your lawyer is coming soon."

"A lawyer?"

"Oh yeah, you gotta pay for beatin' up those cops. You put one in the hospital man."

I can vaguely remember a fight. Dammit. What was wrong with me? I remember being so full of adrenaline. My blood was pumping so hard. I was seeing red. How did that happen?

"Your car is damaged too boss."

Shit. Elizabeth is gonna freak out on me. She was already mad that I purchased a brand-new car without asking her. I don't know how to fix this. I need to talk to her.

"Can I call my wife?"

"Sure thing, but you need to get clean man."

James slides a key into the lock of my chains. "I'm gonna unchain your feet. I can trust you right?"

"Yes sir."

James takes away my chains. He holds them in his hands and stands up.

"Let's go Andrew, you're lookin' better now."

James and I walk side by side down the long hallway.

"You got kids Andrew? Or just a wife?"

I have two sweet little girls boss. They are my whole world."

"Well, let's make sure you get home to them. This ain't no place for you."

James leads me to the row of showers. The tile floor is dingy in the cracks. The faint sound of dripping water hits my ears. The lights are dim. This is what nightmares are made of, even for me, a six-foot boy from the South. Am I gonna be able to go home?

6

I step into the dark shower. I lift my damp shirt over my head. I drape it over the shower rod. There is barely enough curtain to close the shower.

"Yo Andrew, I got you some soap and a towel." James' voice echoes through the line of showers. I poke my head out to see his smiling face. He has a towel and a bar of soap.

"Thank you." I grab my things and drape the towel over the rod. It's brownish yellow and ripped. Better than nothing. I return to undressing. I pull my pants down and lift my leg to get them off. Then I see them. Dug in cuts from having my ankles chained.

I feel like an animal locked away outside. I'm barely holding on in here. I drape the rest of my dirty clothing on the shower rod. I turn on the water straight to hot. A burst of cold water hits me face. It jolts me even more awake. I guess I needed that. As the water slowly gets warmer, I completely submerge myself. I let the beads of water take away all of my filth. The water hitting my face is so refreshing. A smile crosses my face. I'm alive. Thank God I'm alive.

7

"Just a few more minutes boss, we gotta get you ready for the lawyer. What am I facing in here? I gotta get home to Elizabeth and the girls. I can explain everything. There has to be a way to talk my way through this. My heart is pounding. My eyes feel wide. I turn the water off. I'm done. I'm ready to see this lawyer. I'm ready to see my damage.

James leads my half naked body a cell to change. This time there isn't a jail uniform. It's a hospital gown. Interesting. There is a pale green gown, dingy white brief underwear and tan socks.

"They decided you wasn't a threat Andrew." James voice comes up behind me. "Whatever shit you was on when you got here, you better now."

"I'm confused."

"Yeah man, I can tell. Just put that on and take these, you need them." James hands me a toothbrush, a small white comb and a tube of toothpaste.

"Feel free to walk around as you please."

"Really?"

"Oh yeah man, you're good. Make yourself presentable for the lawyer." James walks away to give me privacy. What changed? Just like that, no more handcuffs. No more chains. This feels like an upgrade but is this a hospital? Do I need a gown?

My feet are caked with dirt from the floor. It's pretty tough to get fully clean in here. I sit down on the bed to dry my feet and legs better. I slip on the tan socks. I put one hole of the underwear over my foot. Then the other. I stand up to put my underwear on. Besides the fuzziness in my head, I'm feeling better. I could use some fresh air and another smoke.

I slip the hospital gown over my head. It's a little tight around the middle but it'll work. I'm all set. I turn around to walk out of my cell to see a rusty fork pointed straight at my eye. It's Gavin. Apparently, he wants a piece of me.

Episode 7

1

"Randeep! Hurry man! Come quick!" James and another officer rush over to Gavin and I. Randeep pulls a move I have never seen before and somehow rips the rusty fork from Gavin's hands. James cuffs Gavin's hands behind his back.

"You alright man?"

"Yes sir." I stand completely stunned. There is something utterly scary about Gavin. The look in his eyes. I have never seen a look like that before. He's a monster. I'm left standing, chilled to the bone. I hear screaming and scuffling down the hall. I really need to get out of here. I think James is right. I don't belong in here.

I step out of the cell. I look left. I look right. There is no one around. I feel free in this fortress. I walk away from the shower area and down a long dim hallway. I look up at some light shining through a small round window. Dust has collected on the ledge. Cobwebs are strung around the corners. I see small beads of rain start to hit the window.

The bricks down the hallway are lined with dust. However, the floors are shiny. Freshly waxed. Only a good custodian would notice this detail. My tan socks glide easily across the floor. There is a figure coming towards me.

I see a shaved head. The man has a mint green gown like mine. I can see something dark running down his arms. Is it blood? He is stumbling and mumbling something. Tattoos. It's not blood, its tattoos covering his arms.

2

"He's going to hell!" He shouts. The man stumbles and sits on a wooden bench. I start to walk closer. Drool is dripping from his mouth. "He knows! He knows!" I just keep walking, minding my own business. Surely, it's easy to lose your mind in this place.

I feel like my buddy James is keeping me in check. Strangely, I feel like I have found a friend in him. I am a friendly guy. In my town, everyone knows my name. I get nothing but smiling faces. Just don't mess with my girls and we're good.

Two Teethers and Pumpkin are my world. Daddy will protect them 'til the death. I don't care what I have to do or who I have to go through. They will never do without as long as

Dad's on this earth. I wish Carrie and I were walking up town right now.

We love to walk up and get a nice cold drink and some candy. Just holding hands with my girls feels like heaven. I hear some clicks hitting the freshly waxed floor. They're coming closer.

"Andrew." I hear a familiar woman's voice. It's Monica. I feel a hand on my shoulder. "I'm glad to see you up and about." Monica is breathing heavy. "You scared me. How are you feeling?" Monica gives my shoulder a tight squeeze. I turn to give her a trusting look.

"I'm as good as I can be Miss, I got me a nice shower and some fresh clothes."

"You're looking really good Andrew." Monica exposes a white smile between red lipstick. The smell of her fresh lavender perfume hits my nose. She moves her hand from my shoulder and places it on my lower back. We walk together slowly down the hallway.

"I have a gift for us Andrew."

3

Monica opens her left hand to expose two long cigarettes and a blue lighter. My heart skips a beat. She sure knows the way to a man's heart. A smile crosses my face and my eyes light up.

"That'll work Monica."

"You have really nice blue eyes Andrew. Has anyone ever told you that?"

"A time or two young lady."

Monica lets out a wicked laugh.

"You got two things wrong Mr. Clark."

"Oh yeah? What's that?" I'm being playful and feeling like my old self.

"I'm not quite young and I'm not quite the lady either." Monica is laughing and giving my side a squeeze.

"I beg to differ."

"He's going to pay! He has to pay for this!" The man covered in tattoos yells from down the hall.

"Don't mind him," Monica says with a wink. "He's a lost cause. Unlike you."

We hit the red door. Fresh air and a smoke. There really is a God. And I have good company at that. Monica pulls a set of keys off of her belt loop. She slides a silver key, turns it and pushes the door open. Damp, cool air hits my face. A fresh fall rain just fell. Wet maple leaves cover the ground. I don't have shoes on but I don't mind.

I'm not gonna miss this chance to be outdoors. I live to be outside. Being born in Tennessee and raised in Michigan, I love this weather. I spent my childhood pickin' worms off of tobacco plants and pickin' apples.

4

My mind fades to my Pa. Even though he was the violent angry type, he only hit me once. We were out on the apple orchard. I was making a clicking sound with my mouth and the man I was with was whistling.

"Knock it off," said my Pa. I remember thinking that guy should stop whistlin', my Pa didn't play around. If he told you to do something, you did it. Then I felt the pain. Pa slapped me. He wasn't talking to the other guy; he was talking to me. I haven't made that clicking noise since.

"Andrew? Earth to Andrew." Monica is waving a lit cigarette in front of my face. I grab the cigarette thankfully. I glance at the fence surrounding me. Barbed wire covers the top. I just wanna fly away. I need to escape this. I feel like I screwed everything up. Can I fix this? Can I move on from this?

"You are a good man Andrew." Monica's words break through my thoughts. I reach up and take a puff off my cigarette. The menthol flavor hits my mouth. There is no need to inhale. Smoking is just a product of boredom for me. I blow the cigarette smoke into the cool, damp air.

"Thank you, Monica, that means a lot."

The rusty door swings open and bangs against the building.

"Monica! Come quick!" It's the man from earlier. Randeep is his name? He looks like he's not messing around. Someone screwed up. Monica runs inside and the door slams shut. Huh. Maybe that feller from earlier is in deep trouble. Surely, he didn't mean me any harm. What was he gonna do with a fork? Even though he had a monstrous look in his eyes, he was harmless. He wasn't going to do anything.

5

I take a step off of the cement area and into the leaves and grass. Wetness leaks into my socks. It reminds me of trudging through the backwoods with Anthony. Even though we are ten years apart, we share the same birthday in March.

I wish I could hear the sound of his voice right now. He always reassures me that everything will be alright. I could be lying on my deathbed and he'd say, "Andrew, you'll be alright." He has a thick southern drawl. He lived in Tennessee longer than I did growing up. I'm the youngest of six siblings. I love them all very much. I just want the best for them. I don't wish harm on anyone.

I breath in the Autumn air through my nose. I'll take it. It's better than being inside. To be honest, they could just leave me out here and I'd be just fine. Just keep the food, coffee and puffies comin'. I take a walk over to the chain link fence. I step up and grab the metal with my hand. It's cold with drips of water. I give it a shake just for kicks. It's loose somewhere. I shake it again and look up and down the fencing.

Then I spot it. The chain link fencing is raised up in one spot. I doubt a big boy like me could get out but a smaller guy could. By the looks of the men in here, I don't think we are supposed to be escaping this place.

6

"What do you mean you can't lock him in solitude?"

That bitch Monica has it in for me. You guys can't lock me away forever.

"It's his lawyer, he's fighting it." Good 'ol Dr. Chadwick. My lawyer tells me I need to be rehabilitated. I guess they can't do that if I'm not around the others. It took over. I couldn't listen to the voices anymore. I needed to see blood. It controls me. It has to be Andrew. He will be my next victim. No one can stop it. No needle or pill can take this away. If it doesn't happen, my brain is going to explode. I just can't take the madness anymore. The flesh is the only way to stop it.

"What the hell were you thinking Gavin?" Doctor Chadwick busts through the door.

I jolt in my handcuffs. Being cuffed to a chair isn't the most comfortable position to be in. Can he handle the truth? The fact that I am consumed by consuming my victims.

"Gavin, if you are as innocent as you say you are, this isn't helping your case!"

The doctor is angry. He thinks he's been helping me this whole time. Him and Monica. They genuinely think they can fix me.

"It's the voices, they just take over. I can't control my own body."

The doctor sits down and grabs a notebook and a pen.

"And exactly what did the voices say to you Gavin?"

He can't handle the truth. The monster needs blood and flesh. It doesn't matter. Surely the police are sifting through my apartment right now. There is no way out of this. I can't buy any time. I'm just not ready to face the music. I'm not leaving this place. Doctor Chadwick and Monica can't save me. They can't fix it.

7

"I just blacked out." Doctor Chadwick looks at me with disbelief.

"Go on."

"I blacked out and the next thing I knew, I was in front of him, honest to God." This isn't the first time I've had to lie through my teeth. I had to charm each one of my victims. I am a charming person. No one can deny that. My family always wanted me to use it to gain a wife.

Why couldn't they understand me? No one understands me. Nobody knows the real me. I don't even know who I am. Am I me or the monster? I am him.

"Gavin, we are going to give you another chance. We may have to switch your meds again."

My heart sinks. Dammit! They don't work! Monica loads up a silver tray. There is a syringe, three small orange pills, a large white one and a small cup of green liquid. Over my dead body am I taking all of that.

That's enough to knock out an elephant for a week. This isn't fair. It's inhumane. I start jerking in my chair. They are going to pay for this.

"You can't get away with this! You can't! You can't stop him!" He needs blood and soon.

Episode 8

"Hello, Elizabeth?"

"Andrew, how could you? How could you let this happen? I didn't know where you were for weeks!"

"I don't know, I'm so sorry, can you send me some clothes and smokes?"

"Andrew, did you see the lawyer yet? You are in deep trouble. And that car you bought is totaled. And how am I supposed to pay all of these bills? The girls are asking questions. What am I supposed to do?"

My ears are ringing. I don't know where to start. How do I explain this? I'm still trying to make sense of it myself.

"Andrew, did you know that you are schizophrenic? You kept it from me."

"Elizabeth, I'm sorry. I'm going to fix this." I don't know how, but I will. "Tell the girls I love them."

"Goodbye Andrew."

My ears fall on silence. What happened to love and understanding? Obviously, I didn't do this on purpose. She has to understand. This may seem cliché but I'm innocent. They can't keep me in here forever.

I will get out. I will fix this. I will be back to work in no time. Life will be back to normal. I promise. Standing here staring at the phone, I feel helpless, hopeless. There seems to be no hope in trying.

God, can you show me a sign? Can you help me? I need to see the light.

2

"I know what you did!"

I turn to see two men nose to nose. It's Gavin and the man with the tattoos.

"You won't get away with it, I know."

Gavin is just staring straight through him.

"That's enough Thomas!" Monica swings around the corner. The room is filled with men. Some young, some old. Some are in prison orange jump suits and others in gowns like mine. I guess this is the rec room.

Metal tables are bolted to the floor. Puzzles, dominoes, checkers and chess boards fill the table tops. Then I see it. A ping pong table. No one can beat me at ping pong.

"Thomas, back up!" Neither man moves. Gavin's eyes are locked on Thomas. This doesn't look like it's gonna end well.

"Guards!" Monica yells for backup. "I said guards!"

Randeep and James run around the corner. I wouldn't mess with those boys, they aren't playin' around. I feel so disheartened by conversation with Elizabeth. I need her to know that I'm sorry. I need to speak to her again.

I never meant for any of this to happen. I was in such a great mood that day. What happened? I remember grabbing a burger, fries and a Coke. There was a homeless man. I had just cashed my check from the school. I had fifteen hundred bucks in my pocket. I was feeling great!

I flipped the homeless man a twenty and gave him a pack of smokes. I had a whole carton in the trunk of my beater car. That's when I knew it was time.

3

That piece of junk car had to go man. Elizabeth and the girls deserved a nice vehicle to ride around in. My girls gotta stay safe. Only the best for them. So, I headed to the local dealership. It was almost Pumpkin's birthday. Everyone was going to be so surprised.

My day and mood couldn't have been any better.

"Gentlemen, step away from each other," Randeep says authoritatively.

I wouldn't want him to take action. James reaches towards his belt where he has mace and a night stick. Gavin slowly backs away. Thomas doesn't move.

What is this guy's problem? Obviously, everyone in here is here for a reason. It's no one's fault. Only if I can prove that I didn't do anything on purpose, they might show some mercy.

"Andrew!" Monica is waving a piece of brown paper towel in front of my face. I give her a puzzled look.

"Your mouth Andrew, wipe your mouth." She is talking loud and slow.

I slowly grab the paper towel. I reach up to my mouth with my free hand. Oh. Some drool has collected on the side of my mouth and chin. That's a first. I knew I was out of it, but not that bad.

I give Monica a nod. I'm finding it hard to speak. I can think and feel but my words are lost somewhere in my brain. Monica leads me over to a chair and sits me down.

"Wait here Andrew."

The men in the room are matching my demeanor. Everyone is moving slow. I spot an old man with white hair in a striped gown. His head is slumped down. He appears to be asleep. Is that my future?

Will I be in here until my hair turns white? That can't happen. I gotta fix this.

4

"Andrew, are you able to speak?" Monica is waving her hand in front of my face. I can see her but I can't respond.

"He ain't good to see no lawyer man." My buddy James.

I feel a smile cross my face. He sure does keep me going. My throat is dry. My eyes feel heavy. I have the sudden urge to lie down. I really need some water, and some sleep.

"We'll let the doctor decide that James."

Let James tell you. He should run this place. He knows more than all of you combined. Then silence. I'm left staring off into the room. This is so surreal. This is not happening is it? Me, with all of these strangers. My entire mouth is dry.

Just like magic, water appears in front of me. A bony hand reaches it up to my mouth. I reluctantly take a sip. Can I trust him? Not too long ago, he was holding a rusty fork to my face.

He tilts the cup as I guzzle the water.

"These meds will kill you. They don't give a shit." He obviously understands how I feel. The ice-cold water soothes the back of my throat. I wasn't expecting help from this feller. People surprise me every single day. I've seen a lot in my time on this planet.

"Gavin get away from him!"

5

Monica's shrills pierce my ears. I seem to snap out of it. I look left to see Monica on the defensive.

"It's okay," I manage to mumble. "He's helping."

Monica has a concerned look on her face.

"He needs some food and something to drink," Gavin snaps. "You can't just pump us full of shots and pills on an empty stomach."

I find myself agreeing with the man. I honestly can't remember the last time I've had a meal. It does feel like we are fighting for our survival in this place.

Gavin rips open a bag. The scent of potato chips hits my nose. My favorite. Ever since I was a kid. Gavin holds a chip up to my mouth. He's slightly shaking. I'd be nervous too. I'm a big boy. This guy doesn't stand a chance against me.

I take a bite of the small chip. Grease and salt fill my mouth. My stomach lets out a growl. Just what I needed, I guess. Gavin is staring into my eyes. The look is different than before. His eyes are no longer monstrous. He doesn't look evil or scary.

He has an accepting look in his eyes. Like he understands. A smile crosses his face.

"Can you tell me more about heaven Mr. Clark?"

This boy is dead serious. What changed? I wasn't expecting him to change his mind.

"Tell me everything Andrew." Gavin reaches up with another chip. I guess the world isn't going to end after all.

6

Monica is staring from across the room. She doesn't approve of me conversing with Gavin. She doesn't understand I'm a big boy. I can handle myself. I went through the portal to be here. I didn't do all this for nothin'. I have a destiny to fill.

This young man has come to me for The Word. Therefore, The Word is what he shall receive. Gavin holds another chip to my mouth. I grab it with my hand and take a bite. How did he know that I needed something to drink and some food?

"I have found God Mr. Clark."

My eyes light up. I am happy to hear that. I am always happy when people find the Lord.

"Yo Gavin, it's shower time for you." James comes around the corner with a uniform, a towel and soap. James glances at Monica and she glances back. They don't seem to be buying Gavin's demeanor. I believe anyone can be good if they really want to. Me, even him.

7

He has no clue. I'm coming for him. Mr. Clark. He is the answer for my problems. No one can stop it, not even me. I found God alright. Anything to get me closer to him. I want to hear everything he has to say.

I want to hear his whole life story. Tell me everything Mr. Clark. I really want to know. A snarky laugh escapes me in the warm shower.

"No funny business Gavin."

Sure thing Mr. James. I'd take you out too but you're not my type, sorry.

"James, I need you man, come quick."

Footsteps scurry out of the shower area. Good. A moment of peace I can be alone. I hate always having to be babysat. I don't need to be watched like a little kid. What do they think I am?

I am more than what meets the eye. I have hidden layers of me. Andrew will see them though. All of my victims do. It may be hard to pull off in here though. I can do it. It has to be done. My shower curtain rips open.

"What the fuck Thomas!"

Thomas lunges at me. His hands slip off of my wet body. Really asshole? You're just gonna come at me?

Then I feel it, a sharp pain to my left side. Dammit! Who does he think he is? Then another pain. I'm being stabbed.

"I know!" Yells Thomas. "Everyone knows you're a monster!"

"You don't know me!" I yell in defense. I can feel blood pouring out of my side. I collapse to the shower floor. How? How could this happen?

"No more victims Gavin! You are a sick bastard!"

8

My eyes aren't playing tricks on me this time. That feller is covered in blood. His gown is wet and red. He's standing in the doorway of the rec room. His chest is heaving up and down. He has a sharp tool in his hand.

Good Lord. I jump up and get in a defensive stance. That boy has another thing comin' if he thinks he's gonna roll with me. I'm not gonna hurt him but I'll take him out.

"No more victims!" Thomas yells out. Let's hope so boy. James and Randeep run up behind him and grab his arms. The sharp object falls to the floor. It looks like a homemade scalpel.

Thomas gets whisked away from the rec room. What the hell just happened? All of the sudden the room gets bright. Sirens start wailing through the room. No one moves. No one reacts. Is this normal? What is going on?

"We're on lock down." A voice announces in the room. The man with the white hair doesn't even wake up. This must be typical.

"Andrew, come with me." Monica runs towards me. She looks shocked and alarmed. I slowly get up and follow her to the hallway.

"Did Gavin say anything to you?"

"Just that he wanted to learn more about the bible and heaven."

"That's it?"

"Yes Miss."

"Go back and sit down Andrew. Don't leave this room."

The sirens are still wailing through the facility. What is going on?

Amy Perez MS Psychology

Episode 9

I wake up on a bed of itchy blankets. I feel like I've been asleep forever. I feel comfort. Peace. My mind feels clear. I roll over to see my dark cell. How did I get here? No more sirens. No more chaos. What happened to that feller with the blood? Did I imagine that? The pills they give us sure are strong.

I roll off of my blanket and onto the hard floor. I walk over to use my toilet. I lift up my hospital gown. I feel empty. Hope is lost. I need my family. I try and shake the sadness but I can't. I need them.

"Andrew, let's go man, your lawyer is here."

My cell door opens up. James leads me down a row of cells. I walk into a small room with a wooden table and metal folding chairs. A man in an oversized brown suit and a black comb over stands up. He reaches out to shake my hand.

I reach out and grab his. He motions for me to sit down.

"Have a seat Mr. Clark."

I sit down in a metal chair. It feels cold on my bare legs. Smoke? He reaches over the table with a pack of cigarettes with a red label.

"No thanks." I can't smoke cigarettes that aren't menthol. They make me sick. The man lights up and takes a big drag. He leans back in his chair.

"We're getting you off."

I stare at him confused.

"You were in a psychosis when the officers found you Mr. Clark."

"Is that a good thing or a bad thing?"

2

"Well, in your case, it's a good thing."

A sigh of relief escapes my body. That'll work.

"You're a good man Mr. Clark. It's not your fault that you have a mental illness."

That's a good thing, I guess.

"You will be on probation for a year. And you have to stay on your prescribed medication."

Am I getting out of here? This is too good to be true.

"You will have to visit a psychiatrist once every two weeks. I need you to sign here that you agree."

I pick up a pen and happily sign my name.

"Have a good day Mr. Clark."

I get up and scoot the metal chair back.

"Come on man, let's get you outta here." James motions for us to leave the room.

I'm in disbelief. I barely even remember the court hearing. I could have sworn I was gonna be locked away for life. Especially when the officers took the stand. I had never felt so guilty in my life. I definitely wasn't myself that night.

I had never been in a fight besides rolling around with Anthony.

"We gotta get you to the discharge area."

"That'll work boss."

"Your ride is on the way too man."

Thank God. Hopefully it shows up quick. Is it a taxi? A bus?

"You're one lucky man Andrew."

We come to a well-lit waiting room with fake leather chairs. There is a window that leads to an office that says intake. It is busy with professionals pushing papers and answering phones.

"Have a seat Andrew. You came a long way boss, it's time to go home now boss."

Home. I happily take a seat and stare out the window. Snow is falling on the sidewalk.

3

"Are you ready Andrew?"

"I sure am Monica, thanks for everything. I don't know how to repay you."

"Well, you can take me with you." I let out a laugh straight from my gut. Monica doesn't laugh though. She is dead serious. I feel my face get hot with embarrassment. She's not even phased by what she said.

"I'm a happily married man," I say with confidence.

"I know," Monica snaps.

I don't care who she is, no one is coming between Elizabeth and I. I meant for life when I took my vows. Monica hands me a folded-up piece of paper. I open it to see her name with numbers written underneath. Followed by kisses and hugs. I close the paper in my hand.

"In case you change your mind. I can work in a small town. We could have a life together Andrew."

I'm stunned. Shocked. I never once thought this way about her. I hope I didn't send the wrong messages. The whole time I was here, I had one thing on my mind. Going home to my wife and little girls. I wouldn't throw that away for anything or anyone. Monica slumps her head and turns and walks away.

"Monica."

My dutiful nurse quickly turns around.

4

"Thanks again for everything. Tell James the same for me will ya?"

"Sure thing cutie." Monica shimmies through the doorway back into the facility. I just wanna leave all of this in my past. I wanna forget all about it. I never want to be locked away like this again.

The front doors to the waiting room swing open. Snow blows in from outside. I cannot believe my eyes. It's Dana, Elizabeth and the girls' grandparents. They are all bundled up from the frigid weather. I jump up from my chair. Dana comes running towards me.

"Daddy! Daddy!" She embraces my legs in a huge hug. Elizabeth stands there staring at me. She looks angry and overwhelmed. I don't blame her. She slowly walks up to me then embraces me in a hug.

I am surprised and happy. I return the hug as a tear of pure joy escapes my eye. She gives me a warm smile. My mother-in-law approaches Elizabeth and I.

"Did you know a man was murdered in here?"

Oh geese, good job Grandma. I cover Dana's ears. This isn't a place for a young girl anyway.

"Oh yeah, he was a mass murderer, he ate people Andrew. Did you meet him?"

"Mom!" Elizabeth gives her a disapproving look. She takes a hint and stops talking.

"Don't bring all of that up right now. Let's get him the hell out of here," my father-in-law snaps. He hands me a plastic bag full of clothes and a pair of shoes. I can see my custodian work shirt on top.

"Yes, you still have your job Andrew," my father-in-law says with a smile. "You are a good man."

5

I step into the bathroom with my clothes. I remove the gown and my issued underwear. I feel like a human now. I have dignity. I'm not a criminal or a hospital patient. I slip on my work shirt. My name is stitched over the left pocket. Underneath reads "custodian."

A huge smile crosses my face. I'm a workin' man. Ain't nothin' farther from the truth than that. I don't know how I kept my job but I'm so thankful. I take my light blue jeans out of the bag. Out falls a pair of underwear and socks.

I pick up my underwear and slip them on. Next, my jeans. I step out of the bathroom to sit down to put on my socks and shoes.

"Daddy, you are coming home!"

Dana's voice is pure innocence. I embrace her in a big hug.

"And Pumpkin?"

"She's with my sister," Elizabeth exclaims. "I felt she was too young to take the trip."

I bend down to put on my socks and tennis shoes. I definitely don't mind wearing my work clothes out of this place. A feeling of pride washes over me.

"Let's go everybody."

We all leave the facility together. I zip up Dana's coat all the way and pull her hat down over her ears.

"Bundle up young lady." I grab her gloved hand and walk out. My medicine makes me pretty drowsy; I hope it isn't masking my excitement.

Schizophrenic Episode Series

Episode 10

1

There she is, those blonde pigtails don't get any cuter.

"You ready?"

"Yes Daddy, I'm ready."

"Okay Carrie, bend your knees. Put your bat up." She's ready. I wonder if she's gonna hit it this time. I lightly toss the ball underhand towards my little girl. She swings with all her might. And she misses. Again. Oh well. Maybe someday. I walk towards her.

"No, Daddy, one more time." I let out a laugh.

"Naw, naw, Daddy's gonna take a little break." I take a seat in my lawn chair. I glance down at the grass. It's getting kinda long. Time for a cut. I'll have to gas up the riding lawn mower. The girls can help me pick up the sticks.

Carrie runs over and jumps on the swing. Her summer dress sways in the wind. Dana bursts through the storm door and joins her sister. Daddy's little angels. There ain't nothin' Daddy won't do for his girls.

It's been nine months since I've been out of the maximum-security mental hospital. What a long, hard road. Everyone knows now. Andrew, the schizophrenic. It's hard having a reputation around town. The people that used to smile and wave just walk by without a glance.

It is pretty embarrassing. But at least I'm home with my family. I got my wife and the girls. Oh yeah and too many animals. Elizabeth and I have some things to discuss.

2

"Here you go sweetie." Elizabeth is holding a fresh cup of coffee for me.

"Thank you dear." She pulls up a lawn chair beside me.

"You know they found more bodies."

I glance at her confused.

"Gavin the cannibal. There were two more bodies behind his grandmother's house."

A straight chill shoots up my spine. It takes a lot to spook me but that boy was a piece of work.

"Jesus Elizabeth, don't let the girls hear you."

"Well, you were in there with him Andrew. Did you see him? Talk to him?"

"You don't wanna know, that boy was pretty rough."

"I should write the paper and tell them that you were locked away with Gavin Delaney."

"No Elizabeth."

"Well, we should." Elizabeth lights up a menthol and breaths in hard. She's been through a lot since my hospitalization. She's a good wife.

"I'll take one." I glance at her lit cigarette.

"Get your own," she says playfully. "I just sat down."

"Should we fire up the grill?"

"That sounds good honey." Elizabeth leans back in her chair.

3

"I'm gonna walk up to the corner. I need to stretch my legs." I turn to walk out of the fence.

"Daddy, Daddy, wait for me." Carrie's little legs carry her at lightning speed towards me. I give her a smile.

"No Carrie, stay here," Elizabeth chimes in.

"That's okay honey, she can come with me."

I feel a small hand grab my hand. My little girl and I walk over our stone driveway to the sidewalk.

"Hi Andrew."

"Hi Mr. Clevers! How are you sir?"

"I'm alive."

I burst out laughing and so does Carrie. Our neighbor Mr. Clevers is pushing ninety. At least he treats me the same. He can see that I have a good heart. I can't help that my brain is less than perfect.

My little Pumpkin and I walk hand in hand down the sidewalk. Some candy and juice is in our near future.

Andrew Clark was later diagnosed with bipolar disorder type one. Years later, the diagnosis changed to bipolar disorder type two. As the mental health field progressed, so did Andrew's treatment. Andrew retired as a custodian after working for thirty years. He is now a loving Grandfather. He is known and loved in his community. He spends his time cooking, cleaning and doing yard work. He spends his days helping others every chance he gets.

Schizophrenic Episode Series

A special thank you to everyone who has gone through different treatments of mental illness to contribute to where we are today. Because of you, the mental health field has moved forward in a positive direction. May the field and treatment continue to improve.

Narcissistic Episode

Series

(Preview)

Amy Perez MS Psychology

Amy Perez MS Psychology

Episode 1

1

"Baby! We have new neighbors! And they have kids!" He sure is handsome. My husband. I cannot believe we're married. What a dream come true.

"That's great sweetheart. Oliver will have someone to play with." Mitch grabs the chicken to put it on the grill. This is fancy compared to our usual hot dogs and hamburgers. I swear, I thought we were done being broke. Until Mitch took an internship.

"Baby can you grab the melted butter off of the counter?"

"Sure sweetie." I walk through the sliding glass door. Things will get better, they always do. I peak into the living room to see a zombie. At least that's what I call Oliver when he's engrossed in video games. He is staring the screen with his bright blue eyes. I glance at his blonde hair. It's getting kind of long. I guess I can charge a haircut on my credit card. Oh yeah, butter.

This is a special night. It's Friday. Typically, Mitch would be working nights and weekends in the service industry. But not anymore. He's an intern and he works normal hours. Thank God. This is all I've ever wanted. Oliver and I have spent so many nights, weekends and holidays alone. I walk through the door to see Mitch talking to a man. He is the definition of Caucasian.

He has light skin, blue eyes and dirty blonde hair. He is skinny but muscular. It is a vast difference against Mitch's dark features. Being Italian gives him an authentic look. The men look pretty infused in their conversation. I quietly walk up with the butter and set it on the grill.

2

Ah, the kickoff of spring. This winter was rough and freezing. That's how New York is though. But the city is gorgeous. You just have to take the good with the bad. My family is minutes away. The school systems are great. My husband and I are in great schools. Back to work for me.

I walk into the kitchen and adjust my mannequin. She is wearing a fashionable red top. I should make about fifteen dollars off of it. It isn't what I planned on doing for work. But I can't afford child care in the area. Plus, it keeps me busy. Not that I need it. Studying psychology is pretty tough. My neuropsychology class is kicking my ass.

I snap a few photographs of my mannequin. Hey money is money. It's not forever. Honestly, it's pretty enjoyable. I glare out of the door wall of our townhouse to see the men laughing. Looks like we will get along with our new neighbors. The smell coming in from the grill is intoxicating.

"Baby, come here for a sec." Mitch waves a hand.

3

I pull open the screen door. The screen is hanging off of the frame. The life of having a dog and a cat. I manage to crack a smile. What is it called smiling depression? A great way to hide the pain. I am really good at it. Mitch is able to see right through it though. I do enjoy that he can light a match in my darkness.

"Hi, how are you?" I give a nice smile. "My name is Noelle."

"Chance. Chance Robins."

"Nice to meet you Chance."

His eyes are crystal blue. They seem to pierce right through me.

"You are going to love this area. The school system is great for your children."

"Oh no, they aren't mine."

I stare at him blankly. I don't want to judge or make any cliché reactions. I don't exactly come from the most picture-perfect background myself.

4

"Can I grab you a beer Chance?"

"Sure, that'll be great."

I turn to walk away. That guy doesn't seem super respectful. His demeanor. He definitely feels superior, that is obvious. I grab a Bud Light out of the fridge.

This is the shittiest beer ever. At least for me. It's safe though. Everyone loves it. Should I shake it up? Knock him down a peg? I pulled the prank on my Grandfather when I was about seven. He wasn't too happy. Thank goodness he had a good sense of humor though. I'll play nice, for now. I gently twist the cap off and toss it on the counter.

"Oliver, dinner is almost ready," I call out to my little angel.

"Okay Daddy!" I check the boiling corn on the stove. It isn't quite time for sweet corn yet but it will be pretty good. I poke each corn on the cobb with a fork to get them to spin. Just about done.

I hear Mitch bust out laughing. I just want him to be happy. He deserves the world. Life isn't exactly easy at the moment. However, we are healthy and the weather is finally warm.

5

Personally, I love the snow. I love to play in it with Oliver. I love sipping coffee while watching the snow fall outside my window.

"Here baby."

Mitch reaches out a hand for the cold beer. I'll let Mitch handle Chance. I haven't made my mind up on him yet. Two blonde haired girls come running behind the row of townhouses. Their blonde curls are blowing in the breeze. How cute, I can see a resemblance.

So, what did Chance mean by the fact that they weren't his? Was he kidding? Are they adopted? Mitch and I adopted Oliver when he was a baby. We were so happy. The day that we got approved to be foster parents was the best day of our lives.

6

I don't want to be the nosey neighbor type though. That's not my style. Eventually, I will hear their story. I am really good at getting people to open up. It happens everywhere I go. People just end up telling me their whole life story.

I guess that's why I am in school to become a psychologist. I love to hear people's life story. Plus, I have a family history of mental illness. It just makes sense.

I turn the burner off and cover the corn. It just needs to sit for ten minutes and it'll be done. Mitch and Chance seem to be getting along great. Stop it Noelle. Don't be so jealous all of the time. I hate that about me.

7

That is my least favorite personality trait. I try so hard to hide it. I am always jealous of my sister too. It isn't because she is a woman. It's just that I feel like her and my Mom are closer than I am to them. I know it's dumb. I just can't stop it. It's just like I don't have the same connection. I do like some of the same things as they do. I just don't have enough time for shopping and going out like I used to. Oliver takes up all of my time.

I just love him, I really do. I just never feel like I am enough. I definitely took on the Mommy role right away. Hopefully he isn't confused by having two Dads. Hell, sometimes I'm confused. What should Mitch and I each be responsible for?

I even get jealous if him and Oliver are closer than Oliver and I. Ugh, as much as I want to be a psychologist, I feel like I am the one who needs the help. I plop down on the couch next to Oliver and place my hand on his knee.

"Hey Buddy."

Oliver gives me a glance. Then he stares back at the screen. My little zombie. Good thing he only gets an hour a day.

All of the sudden I hear shattering glass. What the hell? I jump up from the couch to check on Mitch. My fight or flight mode has been activated.

Amy Perez MS Psychology

Episode 2

1

"Babe, he tripped!" Mitch yells from outside.

Chance stands up with a confident smile. Beer is covering his sliding glass door. I run over and grab a paper towel roll. A woman with blonde hair, tattoos and piercings comes around to the backyard. She is fairly straight-faced. She should seem more excited for just moving into a new place. I run over and reach the paper towel over the fence.

"Thanks man, I appreciate it."

"You're bleeding."

Chance looks down at his hand. He doesn't look phased. That's weird.

"Shit." Chance whips open his door and stomps inside.

Mitch grabs the chicken of off the grill as if nothing even happened. How can he be like that? He has such a lack of empathy. Especially for strangers. He seems to only genuinely care for Oliver and I.

He always seems very obsessed with me. He is overly involved in my life. If we get into an argument, he won't even let me walk away. He follows me. Honestly, he scares me sometimes.

He was ordered to take anger management classes when he was a teenager. If it wasn't for my Father, I would probably question him more. My Father loves him. He is always bragging about Mitch. He says that he gained another son the day we got married.

2

"Baby, you gonna help me out?" Mitch is slicing the chicken on a cutting board.

"Yes boss."

Mitch doesn't say anything. He typically doesn't reply to my sarcasm. I feel like one day, he is just going to snap.

I grab a pair of tongs and grab his butt with them. He gives me a side eye. I know he is stressed about the new job. I get it. I'm just trying to break the tension.

"Can you clean up those clothes and your mess?"

Damn. Okay. I wanted to work after dinner but Mr. Clean freak has other plans. He gets it from his Mother. I am a clean person, but damn. They want perfection. It is literally impossible to keep a house perfect. Especially with a young child. He is always experimenting and making messes.

I grab Sally to take her down to the basement. That's the name of my mannequin. My sister taught me to sell clothing online. I named my mannequin after the store that we buy clothing from to resell.

This basement gives me the creeps. It is cold and unfinished. All of the brick townhouses in our row have the same creepy basement. If one floods, then they all flood, it's the worst. I set Sally in the corner. I glance over at Mitch's technology bins. They are off limits to Oliver and I. Mitch is a huge video gamer. He goes live on the computer three times a week. He has gained thousands of followers this year. I am happy for him. And of course. Jealous.

"Babe!"

"Coming!"

I walk up the wooden basement stairs to darkness. What the heck? There are two candles lit on the table. Mitch is standing at the table with roses. I give him a surprised smile.

"They were in my car." Mitch hands me a card. He really is so sweet. I peel open the envelope. It's a thank you card. I start to read the inside. A tear falls from my cheek

3

How does he always do that? He always makes me cry. He is so sentimental.

"I love you." Mitch leans in for a kiss.

Our passion hasn't dwindled in our fifteen years together. We have been through so much and hard times. The worst was when I got diagnosed with manic depression. Even though it was devastating, it was a relief. We finally had an explanation for my behavior.

We found out why I would explode with anger and irritability. It explained my sleepless nights. No matter how bad it got, Mitch stayed by my side. Literally, everyone in my life has either shied away or walked away. Except for Mitch.

We embrace each other in a long hug. Just what I needed.

"Baby, it's Chance."

Mitch backs away. "You're jealous of him?"

"No, it's Chance, he is staring in our window."

Mitch turns to look outside. Chance is standing by his fence glaring in our window.

"Maybe he likes red heads with green eyes." Mitch pokes me in the arm.

"So, not funny!"

"Fuck him, he's a weirdo babe."

How is Mitch like that? Literally, nothing phases him. I am officially creeped out. Does he have a problem with gay people? It wouldn't be the first time we have encountered it.

Oliver comes running into the kitchen.

"Yummy!" He shouts.

Mitch and I bust out laughing. Oliver is so dang cute. He keeps us on our toes, that's for sure.

4

Mitch pulls out a bottle of Meiomi Pinot Noir. It's the wine we bought the night we got engaged. Wow, he is pulling out all of the stops. Shit. He must have to go out of town. Dammit. His new job. He mentioned them having him go to Mexico. It's the worst. But the positive side is that he will bring in more money.

"So, when do you leave?"

Mitch let's out a sigh. "In the morning."

"It's okay, Oliver and I can hang out with my Dad."

"Okay my baby."

Mitch twists open the cap to the wine. The wine glasses are already on the table. Oliver is already digging into his chicken. Mitch put some melted butter in a dish on the side of his plate.

Oliver sure is fancy. I don't exactly want to be left alone with the new neighbor.

5

He gives me the creeps. He seems like the guy that all of the girls drool over but deep down he is really a douche bag. Mitch pours our wine as I take my seat. I am just feeling so grateful for where we are in life. Life really is good.

"Oliver, sweetie, do you want some salt on your corn?"

"Yes please."

"Baby, I'm going live tonight."

"Of course, you are, gotta give the followers some action." I give Mitch a playful wink and smile.

6

Ah, so perfect. I am loving this basement. At first, I thought I could use it to practice karate. But now I know of something better. For now, it will be the new home for my pieces. My puzzle pieces that is. I have built quite the collection. The taste of Jack Daniels and Coke crosses my lips. The sweet taste rolls off of my tongue. I am building the most beautiful sculpture. The female body.

It is going to be a masterpiece. It just takes time. My way of getting the pieces isn't exactly easy. The last one was the fight of my life. I turn on my computer to get started. My research.

Each candidate must be carefully planned out. The skin color must be perfect. These damn camera filters that the girls are using is making it difficult.

I don't mind the challenge though. I have already planned my next piece of my puzzle.

"Hello Jolene." A smile crosses my face. Why is this so exciting? Puzzles are just so exhilarating. Once you find the right piece, you can feel so relieved. The stress just melts away. I hear tiny footsteps upstairs. I better make this quick.

Episode 3

1

"Hello, hello peeps! What's happenin?"

I can hear Mitch being quite the entertainer. We finally found good use for the basement. Besides storing all of my clothes for the store.

"Come on Oliver, let's get you in the bath."

Oliver and I head up the stairs to our bathroom. This isn't the best place to live but it isn't the worst. It has a backyard but it's very small. I've always wanted a big backyard for Oliver to play in. Him and I could kick a ball and chase each other.

Not to mention our dog Boots. He is a beagle boxer. He resembles a boxer more. He has really outgrown this townhouse. I just feel like I failed somehow.

I turn the water to warm in the tub for Oliver.

"Come on buddy, get your clothes off and hop in."

"Will you get in with me Daddy?"

I'm not sure if he is getting too old to take baths with me. I wear my swimming trunks but still, he is getting older.

Oliver started pre-kinder this year. He just turned five in the winter.

"Come on Daddy!"

2

"Okay buddy, hang on." I walk into mine and Mitch's bedroom. Our view isn't too great.

It's of the parking lot and the dumpsters. It is convenient for throwing out trash though. However, Mitch and I long for a condo on the water. It just seems so selfish. I want to give Oliver the best life.

I see a silhouette of a person by the dumpster. Male. Medium build. He is throwing out small tied grocery bags. That's weird. He has like fifteen bags. The man is looking back and forth by the street before he throws out each bag.

The person turns in my direction. Shit. It's Chance. My curtains are wide open. His eyes glare into my window. Don't mind me as I stand here in my underwear staring at you.

3

This isn't exactly the best first impression. I rip my curtains closed. It's his fault. He shouldn't be acting shady by a dumpster.

"Daddy, come on!"

I quickly change into my swimming trunks. I remove my Apple watch and set it on my night stand. Mitch would have a fit if I get it wet. As if I care about that stuff. I would rather have a leather engraved bracelet. Or maybe a seashell necklace.

"Hey buddy." Oliver is waiting patiently by the tub. He has about twenty toys ready for our bath. Mitch doesn't like it. I think its great germ control.

Oliver and I throw all of the toys in.

"Are we gonna play basketball Daddy?"

"Of course buddy."

Our version of basketball is when I throw the toys at him and he has to catch them. Each toy is assigned points in advance. The points range from one to infinity.

"Catch buddy."

"Oh no, I missed."

"That's okay! Try again!"

All of the sudden the door swings open. It's Chance. What the hell?

4

"Hey honey, it's just us," Mitch chimes in. Chance is holding a white electronic in his hand.

"Chance has a carbon monoxide detector for us."

"Oh okay, that's great." Even though it's awkward timing. "You never can be too safe," I chime in. "Ow!" Oliver threw a Lego at my face. "No Oliver!"

"Ten points!" Oliver laughs.

Mitch looks over angrily.

"It's okay," I lie.

I will talk to him about it later. I will save the whole teachable moment for next time. Perhaps when I am not half naked in front of our new neighbor.

Chance removes the hair dryer from the plug and puts in his device. It has a blinking green light.

Mitch and Chance walk out of the bathroom and close the door.

"Oliver, you don't throw stuff at people's faces when they aren't looking. That's not nice."

Oliver looks down into the water looking ashamed.

"Okay?"

"Okay Daddy."

I feel like I spoil him too much because he is an only child. I give into everything. I wonder if I am being too soft. I never even thought I would have a child of my own. Growing up when I was a child, it was unheard of to be gay.

Now, it seems perfectly normal. Thank goodness. Mitch is such a macho man that people never believe him. Until they see me. I am not sure if it's my long red hair or the fact that I am always wearing something pink. Pink is my favorite color.

It wasn't always my favorite. When I was a boy, I loved the color blue, playing sports and playing outside. But one day, I just changed and became a more beautiful version of myself.

"Alright Oliver, let's get out and dry off."

"No, no, five more minutes."

"Okay, but I'm getting out."

Oliver engrosses himself in private play with his toys. I love when kids get lost in pretend play. There is just something innocent about it.

5

Back down to my basement. I have planning to do. Plus, my Jack and Coke isn't going to finish itself. Noelle is quite the Dad. Taking a bath with his son like that. It's cute actually. I wish I could be more like that. More carefree. But I'm not. I'm cold. I only put on a show. My loved and friends see a calm and collected guy. A masculine demeanor. Don't forget my fake smile. Never forget the fake smile. Anything can be hidden behind a smile. Pain, lies, murder.

I click the tab on my computer. Some people shop on Amazon. But me? I prefer Instagram. The women are so beautiful. Surrounded by flowers or lying on the beach. I am always tempted to private message them but I never do. That's how I manage to never get caught. Not a like, comment or follow. However, tempting it might be. I just scroll on through minding my business.

My puzzle piece business that is. It has nothing to do with them. It's all about me in the end. It's my wants and my needs.

6

Living in New York makes things complicated. There are always people everywhere. Thank goodness for traveling. I deliver myself. Hey, I'm a nice guy like that. But my next girl, she's a local. I am taking a huge risk I know. But there is something about her skin. It's so white and porcelain-like.

Her makeup is done just so. It must take her at least an hour. She cares about her appearance. And I care about mine. I choose very carefully. And her teeth, they are perfect. She looks like a famous person. She sort of is famous. She has over three thousand followers. What does that even mean anyway? Will they even notice when she doesn't share a picture of her meal or drinks with friends?

7

I should feel bad for this but I don't. It's been five years since my last kill. I have been so good. My palms are starting to sweat. Social media has come a long way since last time. I used to have to do this old school. I have been practicing stalking down women for two years now. Let's call those women my beta testers. Thank you, ladies. I have it down to a science now. I'm confident. I'm good.

I take a sip of my sweet drink. The ice has watered it down a bit. Just how I like it. I slam the rest of my drink. The alcohol fills my stomach. I grab a cigar out of my pack. It's time to head outside for a smoke. I put in my work.

I close the tab on my computer. Just a little innocent scrolling. No big deal. Goodbye for now Jolene. You will be at karaoke this Sunday and so will I. I will clap extra loud when you sing Gwen Stefani songs. I might even buy you a vodka tonic.

I turn the computer off and head up the wooden steps. What can I say? Life is good. I have it all. I really am a great guy. I walk out onto my back porch and light up my cigar. Someone is sitting in the dark, crying. It's Noelle. Fake smile time.

Made in the USA
Monee, IL
18 June 2020